TABOR EVANS

LONGARM

AND THE WYOMING WILDWOMEN

JOVE BOOKS, NEW YORK

LONGARM AND THE WYOMING WILDWOMEN

A Jove Book / published by arrangement with
the author

PRINTING HISTORY
Jove edition / February 1998

All rights reserved.
Copyright © 1998 by Jove Publications, Inc.
This book may not be reproduced in whole
or in part, by mimeograph or any other means,
without permission. For information address: The Berkley Publishing Group,
a member of Penguin Putnam Inc.,
200 Madison Avenue, New York, New York 10016.

The Putnam Berkley World Wide Web site address is
http://www.berkley.com

ISBN: 0-515-12230-0

A JOVE BOOK®
Jove Books are published by The Berkley Publishing Group,
a member of Penguin Putnam Inc.,
200 Madison Avenue, New York, New York 10016.
JOVE and the "J" design are trademarks belonging to Jove
Publications, Inc.

PRINTED IN THE UNITED STATES OF AMERICA

10 9 8 7 6 5 4 3 2 1

"BLESS MY STARS, IS THAT A GAL YOU'VE BEEN HOGGING TO YOURSELF?"

Longarm didn't even sound testy. "Watch your mouth. Miss Daisy, here, is with me, Bergman."

The Black Swede said, "So I see. We don't have to share the pretty thing with the rest of the crew, as long as you're willing to share her with *me*."

Longarm grimaced. "Hang some crepe on your nose in memory of the dead brain inside. I told you this young lady is with me. But if it's any comfort to you, she ain't with me *that* way and there's nothing you'd be interested to share."

The Black Swede loomed over them with a snub-nosed nickel-plated six-gun in hand as he said, "That tears it. I've had all of your smart mouth I can stand, and now you're fixing to get off my damned train and walk the rest of the way!"

Longarm shifted his weight some to stare thoughtfully past him, observing, "We're doing better than twenty miles an hour right now, Bergman."

The Black Swede laughed with as much warmth as your average fox in a henhouse and declared, "I've seen men jump off a train doing forty and *still* the rascals lived. You aim to jump off like a man or have me toss you off?" He leered, then gave a sudden wild yelp and appeared to vanish into thin air with a mournful wail.

DON'T MISS THESE
ALL-ACTION WESTERN SERIES
FROM THE BERKLEY PUBLISHING GROUP

THE GUNSMITH by J. R. Roberts
Clint Adams was a legend among lawmen, outlaws, and ladies. They called him . . . the Gunsmith.

LONGARM by Tabor Evans
The popular long-running series about U.S. Deputy Marshal Long—his life, his loves, his fight for justice.

SLOCUM by Jake Logan
Today's longest-running action Western. John Slocum rides a deadly trail of hot blood and cold steel.

BUSHWHACKERS by B. J. Lanagan
An all-new series by the creators of Longarm! The rousing adventures of the most brutal gang of cutthroats ever assembled—Quantrill's Raiders.

LONGARM

AND THE WYOMING WILDWOMEN

Chapter 1

U.S. Deputy Marshal Custis Long of the Denver District Court kept up on Wanted fliers, and there were not that many wanted men with flaming red hair worn shoulder length. But Rusty Mansfield had no federal warrants out on him as he sashayed in off the sun-baked street out front and Longarm, as he was better known there in the Parthenon Saloon, was salting a boiled egg to wash on down with cool suds after a long midsummer morn on courtroom duty over at the nearby federal building.

Rusty Mansfield had dared to hire a room at the Tremont House and swagger over to the Parthenon for some of their higher priced chilled beer and better than average free lunch because the murder warrant out on him had been distinctly issued in Wyoming Territory to begin with and, after that, he'd used part of the proceedings from that robbery to buy a whole new seersucker suit and expensive derby. So the man who'd stopped that stage and shot that sort of elderly passenger who'd been slow about producing his damned wealth wasn't much worried about anything but that new barmaid with a mop of red hair to outshout his own as he allowed he'd have

1

bourbon and branch water with his pickled pigs feet on rye.

The redheaded killer made his own sandwich as the gal behind the mahogany built his drink. When he asked Longarm to pass the mustard, he got it, even though he hadn't said please. Life was too short to argue with women or assholes who tried to get anywhere with the same in places like the Parthenon during the noon rush.

The asshole smearing mustard on his pickled pigs feet was telling the barmaid she reminded him of a long-lost friendly she-cousin who'd liked to play doctor in the hayloft, back home in 'bama when, from out of the sun-dazzle into the smoke-filled shade stepped what surely had to be somebody's she-cousin. But she didn't look friendly as all eyes in the Parthenon swung her way in bemused admiration.

For she was sort of country and mighty pretty in her summer frock of floral print calico. A bitty straw boater perched atop her upswept taffy hair. A buscadero gun belt road low around her trim hips. The Navy Colt Conversion that should have been in that underslung holster was in her dainty right hand as she stepped inside in line with Longarm at the free lunch counter to demand, in a high pitched but determined manner, "Which one of you redheaded gentlemen checked into the Tremont House last night as a Mister Thomas Thumb?"

Longarm had forgotten Pop Wetzel, the swamper, and that stockyard foreman they called Quirt had red hair. The mustard-grubber next to him answered, easily, "I signed in under an assumed name in the hopes I'd meet up with someone like you, pretty lady. My wife can be such an old fuss when I—"

That was as far as he got. The pretty lady in calico simply swung the muzzle of her .36-caliber Colt up until it was pointing point-blank at the front of Rusty Mansfield's new ruffled shirt and let him have it, close enough to set said shirt on fire.

Nobody landed on his back as limp as a fresh-dropped cow pat if there was a lick of life left in him. But as he

2

sprawled at their feet on fire the pretty lady was thumbing the hammer of her single-action .36 as if she thought he needed more killing.

So Longarm's big left fist swooped down to grip the cylinder of her six-gun and keep it from turning as he poured his beer over the flaming shirt of the dead man, soothing, "You won and there's no need to make a worse mess, ma'am."

She tried in vain to wrest her six-gun from his grip before she stamped a high-buttoned foot and protested, "Give me back my gun if you know what's good for you, cowboy! For I'd be Deputy Sheriff Ida Weaver of Keller's Crossing in Wyoming Territory and that villain down yonder was wanted dead or alive!"

Longarm grimaced down at the smoldering remains oozing piss and blood into the sawdust spread for just such spills and decided, "I saw you kill him. We can worry about abuse of authority after you show me your badge and warrant, ma'am. I ain't just acting nosy. I am the senior lawman present, and I'll just hand this .36 across the bar for safekeeping whilst I show you my own badge and warrant."

As he gave the gun to the redheaded barmaid and reached under his frock coat, the deadly little thing who claimed to be Deputy Ida Weaver muttered awful things about Longarm's manners as she dug into the sporran-like leather purse attached to the other side of her low-slung gun belt.

He'd just examined her mail-order badge and arrest warrant when the blue-clad form of the burly Sergeant Nolan, Denver P.D., charged in with his own gun drawn to tell one and all to freeze.

Then he recognized Longarm looming above the body he'd just been told about. He lowered his six-gun to ask, "What was he wanted for, old pard?"

Longarm soberly replied, "We're still working on that. I didn't want anything in here but some free lunch. This young lady in calico shot him. She claims she's the law from Keller's Crossing. All I know is what I saw,

3

and she sure as certain cleaned his plow for him.''

Sergeant Nolan smiled uncertainly at the vision in calico to ask, ''Keller's Crossing, ma'am? No offense, but
I don't recall any such a township in the Centennial State
of Colorado.''

She dimpled mighty innocent for a gal who could gun
any man in such a premeditated manner and replied,
''Not Colorado, silly. Up north of Cheyenne in Wyoming Territory. This villain I just caught up with was
wanted for murder and highway robbery up yonder.''

By this time Longarm had gone over the tin badge
and the sort of court order she'd handed him without a
hint of shame. He gave them back to her, for the time
being, as he told her, ''I've seen way better badges ad-
vertised in the *Police Gazette* and a first-year law student
who prepared an arrest warrant that casually worded
would surely get a failing grade. But I reckon that goes
with allowing the citizens of a republic to elect their own
judges. Meanwhile, I asked to see your own peace officer's warrant, like the one I carry, allowing I'm sworn
in and authorized to act as a U.S. Deputy Marshal.''

She looked sincerely puzzled as she told him, ''I don't
know what you're talking about. Undersheriff Rita
swore me in as a deputy with my hand on the Good
Book and Judge Edith allowed her own warrant for the
arrest of Rusty Mansfield, there, was all I'd need when
I caught up with the man who shot my poor old Uncle
Dan'l.''

Longarm and Sergeant Nolan exchanged thoughtful
glances. Nolan was first to say, ''Faith, I know Wyoming Territory gave the vote to the women when they
carved themselves out of Indian Country back in sixty-
nine but don't this sound a little thick and all?''

Longarm tried to sound less sure of himself as he
turned to the self-styled deputy sheriff to ask, ''Are you
saying this man you just gunned in cold blood was a
personal enemy before a lady undersheriff deputized
you, right informal, to serve that arrest warrant made out

4

by a lady J.P. who should have known better, across a state line?''

Ida Weaver nodded sort of smug and told him, ''They both agreed a woman with a good motive for bringing that brute to justice might do a better job than any man merely out for the bounty.''

''What bounty?'' asked Longarm, adding, ''There was nothing in that tersely worded scribble about any reward money posted on that poor mess on the floor.''

Longarm turned to Sergeant Nolan to grumble, ''Her so-called arrest warrant was made out by somebody signing E. P. Keller, J.P., authorizing the bearer to track down and bring back one Rusty Mansfield, true name unknown, dead or alive on unspecified charges of highway robbery and murder most foul.''

Sergeant Nolan stared thoughtfully at the smug little gal from north of the U.P. tracks to marvel, ''And did they, now? This would be the first I've ever heard of a justice of the peace having such grand powers, and while I've seen *reward posters* offering bounties dead or alive, I've yet to see any *arrest warrant* worded to read that way!''

Longarm nodded and said, ''I'd be proud to write you up for an assist if you'd see about getting this possible interstate-want over to the morgue for now, Nolan. It ain't that I'm too lazy. But I somehow feel my superiors over to the federal building would rather I brought Deputy Ida, here, in to thrash this confusion out with them.''

Ida Weaver protested, ''You can't arrest me! You can't! I haven't done anything wrong! That beast I just shot down, like the dog he was, did the very same thing to my poor old Uncle Dan'l.''

She must have meant it. She kicked the limp corpse, hard, before Longarm could take her gently by one arm and softly tell her to cut that out, adding, ''I'll take your word, for now, about him being a beast. What separates us human beings from the rest of the beasts is that we try to follow the law of the land instead of the law of the jungle. I know what it feels like to go after outlaws

5

who've hurt kith or kin. So I ain't saying nothing might have possessed me to just blow away a killer I had the drop on. I wasn't *standing* in your shoes when you just done it. I was a good two feet away. I might have some of this situation wrong. But, right or wrong, I have to carry you over to the federal building with me, now. You ain't under arrest, unless you refuse to come along ladylike.''

So she, her still-warm six-gun, and the childishly written arrest warrant came along ladylike, and in no time at all Longarm had her seated in the only chair on their side of the cluttered desk in the smoke-filled oak-paneled office of Marshal William Vail of the Denver District Court.

Billy Vail had been younger and slimmer when he'd ridden with the prewar Texas Rangers. He was still a keen-eyed lawman despite being somewhat older and way dumpier than he'd put up with in even a senior deputy. He'd asked the lady's permit to go on smoking as Longarm, standing by her leather chair, did most of the talking. It was up for grabs whether the crusty Billy Vail would have really put out his pungent black cigar, had anyone asked him to. But as Longarm went on talking, trying to make Ida Weaver sound as kindly as he could, but all too aware she didn't have much going for her, he saw old Billy seemed almost pleased with his account of what could only add up to a murderous abuse of dubious authority.

Vail seemed to brush aside the informal deputization of a known grudge holder as he beamed at Ida Weaver to say, ''You sure tracked him good, Deputy Weaver. You say that before that rascal murdered a kinsman and inspired you to become a law lady, you were running a hat shop and just plunking at cans now and again with a late husband's old six-gun?''

She sighed and said, ''This gun belt was Ralph's, as well. When we moved out to Indian Country from Ohio, he thought it might be a good idea to teach me how to handle a gun.''

Billy Vail glanced at Longarm and chortled, "There seems to be no argument about that. I was more concerned with how a young widow with a hat shop tracked an owlhoot rider on the run all the way down here to Denver and the Parthenon Saloon, of all places."

She confided, "They told me at the Tremont House he liked the free lunch at the Parthenon, and ever so many people on the streets were willing to direct me there from the hotel."

Longarm quietly told her, "He meant how did you track Mansfield to the Tremont House. I know the Overland Feeder Line still stops East-West coaches on Tremont Place, and you told us Mansfield stopped stages for fun and profit, but wasn't that still stretching some?"

She shook her head and answered, "Nobody had to guess. We got a tip about him staying there, signed in as Thomas Thumb, the sarcastic thing!"

Longarm asked if she had any notion who might have tipped off the law in Wyoming when the Denver P.D. was so handy.

She said she had no idea. Before Longarm could ask any further questions, Billy Vail hushed him with a wave of his cigar and rose to his feet, saying, "I reckon we have it figured tight enough, Deputy Weaver. The women having the vote in Wyoming Territory, it was sure to come to pass that one or more counties had to wind up with a sort of girlish complexion, no offense."

Longarm stared thunderghasted as Vail stepped out from behind his desk to lead the way and held out a pudgy hand to help the deadly little thing from her seat, agreeing, "Rusty Mansfield shot an uncle on you. So Justice of the Peace Edith P. Keller made out a dead-or-alive arrest warrant on him and Undersheriff Rita Mae Reynolds swore you in as a she-deputy and told you where to go to serve it on the lowlife, right?"

She said that was what she'd been trying to tell everybody all along. Billy Vail helped her to her feet and led her to the door as he called out ahead.

When old Henry, the young squirt who played the

typewriter out front, came running like the eager pup he seemed to be, Billy Vail told him, "I want you to type something up that this law lady can show any local copper badges out to make a fuss about her showdown with an outlaw here in our jurisdiction. She'll explain as you make it short and simple, Henry. I'll give you her more formal statement after I've had time to decide how she wants to word it. She ain't had as much experience writing up arrests. So as soon as you're done, out front, I want you to escort her on over to Union Station and see her safely off to Wyoming, hear?"

Henry never argued with Billy Vail. Henry was no fool. But as the two of them left, Longarm demanded, "How come you just got so easygoing, Boss? That tale she told sounded sort of wild to me."

Vail waved him to the vacant seat and moved around the desk to resume his own as he growled, "You ain't *heard* wild yet. I get to read more reports from other parts, stuck here like a broody hen whilst you young squirts have all the fun."

He leaned back in his own chair, blew smoke out both nostrils like a proddy bull, and continued. "Eight, that we know of for certain. Eight known but not really famous riders of the owlhoot trail who wound up in the same dismal condition when they were tracked down by wildwomen from Wyoming. Each and every one green about the law as well as girlish. Each one packing a mail-order badge, a half-ass arrest warrant, and a personal grudge against the deceased."

Longarm whistled softly and decided, "I give up. Do you figure some sort of conspiracy or pure shithouse luck on the part of some girlish new hands at the game?"

Billy Vail shrugged and said, "Don't know yet. I'll just have to wait until you tell me, won't I?"

Chapter 2

Longarm had seldom found it profitable to argue with
Billy Vail, either. But he pointed out and Billy Vail
agreed it might look as if he were following Deputy Ida
Weaver if he caught the same afternoon train to Cheyenne. So that gave Longarm another evening in Denver
and old Billy smiled dirty as he told Longarm to give
his regards to a certain pretty widow woman up to Capitol Hill.

Longarm didn't think it was anybody's business that
he was in the doghouse at that address for balking at
attending the same fool opera he'd escorted her to the
summer before. For she was a swell playmate and they
got to nibble and sip whilst sitting up yonder in her
private opera box. But a man had to draw the line somewhere, and it got tedious as all get-out when the same
fat lady in armor kept singing the same song in High
Dutch at the top of her fat lungs.

Had he been in *less* trouble up to Capitol Hill, he still
might have preferred the company of the best lawyer he
knew by quitting time. For he'd gotten out of some more
tedious courtroom duty that afternoon by boning up on
all the telegrams and letters Billy Vail had amassed on

Wyoming wildwomen, and he felt the need for some legal advice.

Portia Parkhurst, attorney-at-law, was neither the best lawyer nor the best-looking woman Longarm knew. But he felt no call to kiss old Judge Dickerson, and the beautiful Miss Fong at the Golden Dragon hardly spoke enough English to discuss legal matters worth mention.

Portia Parkhurst, attorney-at-law, was a tad flat-chested and a mite long in the tooth, but still better-looking than most distaff members of the Colorado Bar Association.

It couldn't be helped. There weren't that many gals in any bar association. Gals had been allowed to *study* law at least as far back as the Portia that Portia Parkhurst was named after. She'd told Longarm her momma had been inspired by that lady lawyer in that play about merchants in Venice. But no state bar association had accepted women, with or without law degrees, before they built the transcontinental railroad and Wyoming Territory in '69. It had taken them until more recent before the higher courts would hear a case argued falsetto by a shemale. So Portia Parkhurst had spent a heap of her professionable career clerking for male lawyers, and if it showed as whisps of silver in her severely bunned black hair, she'd still read way more law books than a heap of slick-talking courtroom dandies.

He'd noticed that on courtroom duty, where they'd met whilst she was defending a train robber he was riding herd on. She'd gotten the guilty son of a bitch off, and they'd naturally gotten to talking it over afterward, having supper together at Romano's and then somehow winding up at her place over on Lincoln Street. She'd been a good sport about him not spending the rest of the weekend yonder, too.

But when he ambled over to her office before his usual quitting time, he found old Portia ready to leave for the day her ownself, and looking severe, even for her, in summer-weight black gaberdine and veiled black hat with black silk roses growing out of it.

10

When they almost bumped noses in her vestibule, he tried to kiss her casually, and when that didn't work he asked her who's funeral they were headed for.

She pulled away, saying, ''I've just come from a probate hearing, and I look silly in a black frock coat. It's very flattering to be taken for any old port in a storm, Custis. But I've had a long hard day, and I was planning to spend the evening alone with a good book.''

Longarm nodded soberly and suggested, ''*Bricks Without Straw* by a new writer called Tourgée would surely qualify as a good book, Miss Portia. But Mark Twain's *A Tramp Abroad* might make you laugh more.''

''Where do you think you're going?'' Portia demanded as she locked her front door, turned away from the same, and found him in step with her.

He answered, simply, ''We both have to go down the same hall and take the same steps down to Wazee Street, don't we?''

She sniffed and said, ''I suppose so. But I frankly don't want to be seen in public with you any more, Custis. I know I lost my head that time and I know what you must think of me, but I didn't know about you and that runaway orphan girl, then, and . . . Don't you have *any* shame?''

He steadied her elbow on the steep stairs whether she wanted him to or not as he replied in a tone of sincere indignation, ''I never told you I was no angel when I said I admired the way you sucked up Eye-talian noodles, Miss Portia. But that runaway I took away from a more shameless cuss after I'd whupped him fair and square wound up out to the Arvada Orphan Asylum, supervised and chaperoned more than most young gals her age. That's because I took her out there and signed her in, pure as I found her, even though she kept trying to tempt me with mighty shocking suggestions, coming from a twelve-year-old.''

The lawyer gal who'd never see forty again sniffed and dismissed his defense with, ''It's so good to hear you didn't think you could fit that thing in a twelve-year-old. I meant what I said, at the time, when you put it in *me*! But that was then and this is now and I'll be damned if I'll let any man use me as no more than a slight improvement on his own hand.''

Longarm sniffed back and tried, ''I don't know what gives you gals the right to take so much for granted. Where do you get off thinking I came all the way across town to play slap and tickle with you, just because I let you have your wicked way with me that one time?''

She laughed, despite herself. But by then they were out on the walk and she insisted, ''I have to be on my way, and I don't want you to follow me, Custis!''

He shrugged and said, ''Suit yourself. I reckon I can find another lawyer to tell me about death warrants issued by a justice of the peace.''

That worked. She turned to stare up at him with a puzzled smile as she replied, ''That's ridiculous. No J.P. has the right to *try* a criminal case. So how could one sentence anyone to more than the fees and fines allowed under civil codes?''

Longarm said, ''I was hoping you might be able to tell me. I came to you with the problem because there's this shemale justice of the peace handing down arrest warrants, directing the server to bring the defendant in dead or alive.''

Portia shook her black silk roses wildly and sounded sincere as she said, ''The presiding judge of a federal district wouldn't word an arrest warrant that way. Lord knows I've read enough of them, and more than one poor cowboy gone wrong has been shot by the law when he wouldn't come quietly. But a J.P.? Before trial in any criminal court? You say another *woman* has been trying to issue such ridiculous court orders, Custis?''

He said, ''Edith Penn Keller, J.P. and she ain't been *trying*. She's been *doing* it, and so far eight men have wound up dead instead of alive. I know you'll say they doubtless had it coming, but—''

''We'd better talk this over.'' Portia sighed, adding, ''Let's hail a ride and go to my place. I meant what I

12

said about being seen with such a rascal in public, but I'll whip us up some supper while you tell me more about this crazy woman who thinks she's a J.P.''

So that was where they went, and Portia served him some swell pork chops and hash browns along with collard greens that he shoved around in the plate to be polite as he told her, ''I came to you about her because a he-lawyer I just talked to back at my office seemed to be as fuzzy as myself on this women's suffering up Wyoming way.''

She rose to produce some marble cake from a bread box on a side board as she dryly remarked, ''*Suffrage* is the word I hope you meant, and I suspected all along you came to me because I was a *she*-lawyer. What's wrong with women being allowed to vote and even hold public office in Wyoming Territory? A republic that denies the vote to over half its adult citizens is by definition not a republic!''

He held up both hands in surrender as he protested, ''Don't look at me! I'm only paid to enforce the laws as others write 'em, and I read what Miss Susan B. Anthony wrote about them fining her and them other ladies for trying to vote for or against Grant in seventy-two! If it was up to me a gal who could read and write would have the vote over any man who couldn't, and vice versa. But, like I said, it ain't up to me, and what I was hoping you could tell me was how come Miss Susan B. got arrested for voting in seventy-two if women have been allowed to vote and hold office since sixty-nine up Wyoming way?''

She served the cake and poured more coffee as she sighed and told him, ''You just answered your own question, Custis. Whether they were listening to their wives or bucking for statehood by registering all the voters they could manage, the founding fathers of Wyoming Territory extended the franchise to all adult white women as far as township, county, and territorial elections and public offices go. Susan B. and her fellow sufragettes didn't try to vote in Wyoming. They weren't exactly arrested for trying to *vote* anywhere. They *registered* to vote at various polling places by signing in under just their initials or in some cases assumed names. They were arrested when poll watchers spotted them standing in the voting lines in their skirts.''

Longarm tasted his marble cake, found it sweet but stale, and took a sip of coffee to help him get it down before he asked, ''Then you're saying Wyoming gals will get to vote for our next president as well as the J.P. of Keller's Crossing?''

She said, ''Don't be silly. I just told you they only get to vote on local matters. That justice of the peace and the very governor of the territory have to be appointed from on high.''

He asked how high for whom.

She thought and said, ''Washington appoints territorial governors and, as you know, federal judges and the U.S. Marshals who back them up by enforcing their rulings. Local voters elect their township and county officials. But it's usually the county board of supervisors who appoint a justice of the peace to serve each township. Circuit or presiding judges are usually elected, but this rather puffed-up crossroads J.P. of yours is probably the wife or play-pretty of somebody on the county board.''

Then she polished off her own cup to add, ''Can I ask *you* a legal question now? Why on earth are they sending you of all people all the way to Wyoming Territory to look into such girlish behavior? Don't they have a federal court in Cheyenne and haven't they any U.S. marshal's office assigned to the same?''

Longarm nodded and said, ''They do. Cheyenne was asked to look into them Wyoming wildwomen after the third killing, over Nebraska way. So Cheyenne said they would. Then they said they had. They said nobody's been able to see anything wrong with Keller's Crossing, a township on the North Platte surrounded by grass and cows, save for the girlish way the trail town's been run with most of the menfolk busier out on the open range with all them cows.''

He took another sip and continued. ''The county and town boards are about three-quarters shemale and one quarter gents with time in town to spare. Cheyenne says nobody in them parts has any complaints about their elected or appointed officials. Things have been running smooth, save for an unusual number of outlaws from other parts passing through what amounts to nothing much. Cheyenne says it ain't unusual to have outlaws passing through a river crossing near the junction of east-west and north-south trails with a short-line railroad spur.''

He drained his cup and added, ''The attorney general, among others, thinks Cheyenne's been sort of casual about that many transient outlaws passing through one prairie township with such fatal results. I wish I had a nickel for every crossroads magistrate who never went to law school. But eight dead-or-alive warrants, served so strict, does seem a mite thick. But she *would* have the power to arraign or order anybody arrested on any charge bound over to a higher court.''

Portia poured more coffee, as if it was all right for him to stay a spell longer, as Longarm continued. ''She'd be in trouble if ever she tried to preside over a murder trial. But old Billy says heaps of small town J.P.s and unpaid hardly qualified town drunks with mail-order badges arrest and start the wheels of justice moving on serious outlaws. So this here undersheriff who keeps deputizing young gals is within the law as well, barely. A citizen who packs no badge at all has the legal right to arrest any felon wanted for any crime, provided he ain't afraid of getting sued if he can't make it stick.''

He smiled thinly and observed, ''Hard to sue a girlish deputy when she's just blown your brains out. Hard to keep her from doing that to you when you're a man on the run, braced for a showdown with somebody coming at you dressed more manly.''

He sipped some of his fresh serving and observed,

"Neither Billy nor anybody else in pants has thought to study on what's starting to bother me. The French say a lawman should start with a *cherchez la femme*. But I've notice that when *femmes* start acting peculiar it might be time to scout for some *hommes*. That's what the Frogs call sneaky men, *hommes*."

Portia allowed she knew all about sneaky men getting her own kind in trouble and got up from the table again as she added, "It seems a bit warm in here despite the jalosie slats in my window blinds. Why don't you hang up that stuffy frock coat and clumsy gun belt while I slip into something cooler."

He allowed he would as Portia left him alone in her kitchen for the moment. He hung his coat over his cross-draw rig, next to the brass hook that was already holding his telescoped Stetson. Then he got rid of the foolish shoestring tie they made him wear on duty in town. For it wasn't as if he was on duty in Portia Parkhurst's warm kitchen. Bless her hospitable hide.

Then he saw how hospitable old Portia's hide could be as she came back into her kitchen, naked as a jay with her silver-streaked hair let down in a vain attempt to shield her still-firm breasts from his admiring view.

He rose to the occasion, both ways, but wasn't sure what he was supposed to say on such a surprising occasion. So he just took her in his arms and kissed her, French, as she shoved him back until his rump was half seated on the table. He had to hold her with both hands to keep her from falling backward as she threw first one leg, then the other, atop the table to either side of him. So she reached down between them to unbutton his fly as a cup, saucer, and some silverware crashed to the floor behind him.

He decided he didn't mind if *she* didn't mind what they were doing to her own tableware. Then she'd hauled out his raging erection to guide it into place as they both wound up atop the table, doing lots of things a kitchen table was hardly intended for.

16

Chapter 3

They naturally wound up in her bedroom to do more natural things in her four-poster, with all his duds off as well. Longarm felt no call to remind her who'd started it that other time. Older women who preferred to live alone but loved to screw were inclined to recall the seduction, as they liked to call it, as the man's sneaky surprise.

So Longarm wasn't surprised, within the hour, to hear Portia sigh about her own lack of willpower as she sat astride him, bouncing as bare as a horse trader's lies, whilst he just took his beating like a man.

Not wanting to be rude, Longarm grinned up at her tossing mane and bobbing breasts to observe, "You're right. There's hardly a male who wouldn't seduce a snake if he could get somebody to hold it's head. You ladies would have to be born with our mean old peckers to understand our wicked ways with a maid. Having nothing betwixt your own legs but them shy and delicate ring-dang-dos must leave you all in the dark about such feelings, huh?"

She leaned forward to brush his mustache with her nipples as she bounced faster, growling, "Shut up! I'm coming and I'll never forgive you for getting me this hot, you brute!''

That made two of them, again. So Longarm rolled her over on her back and hooked an elbow under either of her knees to spread her open wider as she protested, ''I was doing just fine, *my* way, and you know I like to be in control, damn you!''

He growled back as friendly, ''I thought you wanted to shut up and just fuck. Your way was taking too long, and it says in the Good Book that I get to be the boss!''

That pissed her off. He'd known it would. He'd meant what he'd said about folk with different plumbing having a tough time following each other's drift. But he had noticed in his travels that independent women who loved to make love seldom made it to middle-age, unmarried, and downright bossy, unless they turned a deaf ear to the usual romantical mush most men used on great lays. A farmer's daughter or overworked waitress wanted to hear a man saying he'd take her away from whatever. But a gal who'd hung her own law shingle up to charge as much or more as any other top lawyer in town needed to be reassured no mere mortal man was after anything but her swell ass. He suspected he'd let himself in for that last tongue lashing by offering to come by her office that weekend to carry her over to the beer garden for some May wine. This time she knew he was leaving town, come morning. So she'd likely take it dog style, if he just rolled her over and got her into position without saying anything too sweet.

As he rolled off her to roll her over, she asked what he thought he was doing, even though she didn't really resist as he proceeded to do it, saying, ''I've been thinking of the other wildwomen up Wyoming way and how some other long-donging brute might be leading them down the primrose path. I mean, you're a woman, Lord love you, and would you just grab a gun and traipse over to the county sheriff's to get deputized and light out after any outlaw without even changing to a sensible riding habit?''

Portia raised her still girlish rump as she grasped the full intent of his hands on her hip bones and his questing shaft parting her moist pubic hair, observing, "You said all those distaff volunteers were deputized to track down men who'd wronged them or someone in their own families. You're not going to try and put it in the wrong hole, are you, dear?"

He said, "Not unless you ask, polite. Billy and me don't find it logical to deputize inexperienced young ladies to send poking after wanted men."

She said, "Oooh, I want *that* man right where you're shoving him! But why are we talking about poking anywhere else?"

He got it all the way in and began to play her pussy like a trombone in three-quarter time as he demanded, "What makes them gals such good trackers? I mean, sure, anybody can see how a gal might want to go after the man who gunned her dear old uncle. I was there. So I can tell you how easy it is for a gal wearing skirts and a girlish smile to get the drop on a man who'd been running from other men. But then she told me and Billy Vail she'd *tracked* Rusty Mansfield all the way to the Termont House in Denver and from there to his favorite saloon. How in blue blazes do you figure she did that without no help from an experienced manhunter?"

Portia moaned, "Oh, Lord, I know I could sure use more help from an experienced manhunter they call Longarm! I have no idea how some silly cowgirl or schoolmarm might go about tracking down a wanted man. I want *you*! All of you! For I told you the last time you abused me this way that your arm isn't the only thing about you that seems to be unusually long!"

He laughed and pounded her to glory with his bare feet braced on the rug beside the bed, then hauled back on her angular hip bones to hold her firm buttocks against him as he tried to sort of wipe her ass with his belly hairs while she reached back to fondle his puckered balls until he was suddenly draining them inside her. She called him a bastard for not waiting for her

19

when she felt his discharge seeping out over her turgid clit. Then she was calling him nicer things as they lay sideways with him still spooned inside her while he strummed her love-slicked banjo from behind with his skilled right hand in her lap, murmuring in her ear, "One of them Wyoming wildwomen might have gone this far with an outlaw before she shot him point-blank in a Santa Fe posada. That report allows they reported him taken dead in his long underwear. The Mex posadero who hired them both the room was unable to give further details."

Portia arched her spine to swallow another half inch or so of his semi-flaccid shaft as she murmured, "Ooh, don't stop and don't do it any faster. That feels just lovely and I want it to last forever. I'd have to come and cool off quite a bit before I shot you, right now, if you were a wanted man and I was after you with a dead-or-alive warrant from some silly Wyoming J.P."

He kissed her behind one ear and went on pleasuring her as he replied, "I know I'd deserve it, taking up with a strange gal when I knew I was wanted dead or alive and then not keeping an eye on her. But how do you reckon you tracked me all this way from Wyoming, you sentimental little deputy gal?"

The lady lawyer giggled and said, "I'd be a big fibber if I told you I've never had a man pet me so sweetly down there. But I must say I'm not used to speculating on law enforcement, or the lack of the same, at times such as this! You really *do* value my opinions as a lawyer as well as my weakness as a woman, don't you?"

He nibbled her earlobe, her well-kept hair smelled she-male as hell, then assured her, "I cannot tell a lie. I mostly wanted you the way I'm holding you right now. But I told you over to your office I needed a natural woman with a law degree, remember?"

She murmured, "I remember, and I'm so glad, right now, that is. I know I'm going to hate myself in the morning. But you did say you'd be on your way to Wyoming's Cow Country by then and . . . Could we do this *right* some more, Custis? I can always play with that thing *myself*!''

He said they sure could, and they sure did, with two pillows under her shapely but sort of lean hips as she locked her ankles around the nape of his neck and warned him she'd never forgive him if he ever stopped.

Of course, there came a time when he had to, because he couldn't come any more. So whether she forgave him or not, Portia seemed as willing to share a three-for-a-nickel cheroot and let her throbbing flesh cool off a spell as they cuddled atop the covers in the lamplight spilling in from the front room.

Longarm blew a thoughtful smoke ring at the open doorway before he asked her how she'd go about defending someone such as Deputy Ida Weaver when, not if, she got her fool self arrested by shooting the wrong man in cold blood.

Portia absently replied, ''I think I'm jealous. Why do you and all those other lawmen *care* about a girl with a gun and a mind of her own treating killers the same way the rest of you like to?''

Longarm grimaced and said, ''Nobody with a lick of sense *likes* to gun another human being. We generally give them a change to surrender, and *then* we get to gun 'em. To begin with, it ain't always clear a man is guilty as charged before he's stood trial before a judge and jury. That's why them dead-or-alive warrants on men who ain't been indicted have so many cautious thinkers worried. I say when, not if, because as sure as you're concave where I'm convex, a Wyoming wildwoman suffering delusions of deputization is sure to blow away some innocent cuss, and then where will we be?''

Portia replied without hesitation, ''She'll be in a whole lot of trouble! But, since you asked, I think I'd plead her not guilty by reason of orders from higher authority. You did say she was able to show you a valid arrest warrant, or at least a writ that read like a valid arrest warrant, didn't you?''

Longarm said, ''I did. Billy Vail says the one we saw

21

might stand up in court as long as the cuss she served it on was guilty. Rusty Mansfield would have had grounds for damages against little Ida, her undersheriff, that J.P., and Keller's Crossing if he'd live to prove he was innocent! Your turn."

Portia took a deep drag on the cheroot, handed it back to him, and let fly some smoke signals a Kiowa might have bragged on before she decided, "Try it this way. An out-of-the-way Wyoming county might save a lot on courtroom expenses if they recruited unpaid volunteers to simply smile pretty at no-goods and mow them down. What did they call that bunch of young gun waddies Uncle John Chisum and his trading partner, McSween, swore in as unrecognized but efficient lawmen back in seventy-eight?"

"Regulators," Longarm replied, adding, "They didn't work out all that efficient. Both factions in the Lincoln County War wound up flat busted, and they say Billy the Kid was last seen washing dishes down in Shakespeare near the border. After that, this undersheriff Rita Mae Reynolds ain't stuck with the situation Uncle John was, with the county run by a rival faction and his cows vanishing into thin air. Like I said, less than half the elective positions in the township are held by the menfolk of the womenfolk who seem to have grabbed the rest. But they've other J.P.s and Rita Mae works under a male county sheriff, who's yet seen fit to deputize any ladies to go after anybody charged as a felon by Justice of the Peace Edith Penn Keller of Keller Township."

Portia suddenly laughed and said, "I think this must be what some of my married friends mean when they mention pillow conversations. I'm lying in bed with a naked man, still wet with his passion as I snuggle my naked flesh against his, and I'm talking about small-town politics?"

He snuggled her closer and asked how she felt about that so far. She chuckled and said, "Depraved. I'm supposed to be locked in my bath, weeping in shame be-

22

cause I let you touch me in such vulgar ways. But since you ask, I do find it odd that this rather drastic lady's club seems to be dominated or even partly dominated by a woman who has her own division of her county named after . . . whom? Her father or her husband?''

Longarm said, ''I don't know. That's one of the things Billy Vail wants me to look into. As far as we know, none of the younger gals sent out of the territory to gun men down in cold blood in other parts of the country are married up. I for one would be mighty surprised to learn any man with hair on his chest would allow his woman to pin a badge on and go chasing after other men with any aim in mind.''

Portia sniffed, allowed that was how come she preferred to remain a spinster, and pointed out by asking, ''Then it's safe to assume none of the male officials of this remote rural community are too opposed to whatever that small clique of gun-slinging bloomer-girls may be up to?''

Longarm shook his head, put the smoke back to her lips, and told her, ''Nobody in Wyoming Territory seems to give a hoot, male or shemale. Like I said before, crime is down, it's an election year, and no registered voter's ox has been gored. So what the hell.''

She passed the cheroot back, lightly asking, ''What the hell indeed? I can see why the Cheyenne District Court doesn't seem half as interested as your own nosy Billy. Speaking as a lawyer, and don't you dare think I want you to spend even one more night with me, you brute, I can tell you what you're going to find when you arrive up there in that tightly knit community. You're going to cast your questions in deep water and reel in bare hook after bare hook. If even Cheyenne had received one complaint from one concerned citizen of the town or county, male or female, Billy Vail wouldn't have to send you all that way on such a fool's errand, Custis!''

Longarm sighed and replied, ''I told you it wasn't Billy Vail's grand notion. He's passed on orders from higher up. I don't doubt the federal lawmen out of Cheyenne reported just what they'd seen and heard, after they'd seen and heard nothing much. I've been places where nobody talked much to outsiders about the comings and goings of insiders. I've usually discovered that when anything really dirty was going on, I could get somebody to tell me about it, off the record.''

Portia took the cheroot away from him and snuffed it out in a bed table ash tray as she pointed out, "What might you and your Denver District Court be able to do about it if you *do* uncover some sort of fiendish female plot against wanted criminals? People *want* killers killed, Custis. The double-jeopardy hanging of Jack McCall for the murder of Wild Bill Hickok was unconstitutional but just, as far as anyone ever cared!''

To which Longarm could only reply, "Jack McCall must have cared, and I'm sworn to uphold that constitution. I don't hold with lynch law or vigilante justice, Miss Portia. So I reckon I'd best get on up yonder and file a full report on just what's been going on, constitutional or otherwise. I'll come by to tell you which, as soon as I get back.''

Portia forked a long bare leg across him to once more impale her lean but tender flesh on the boner she was gripping with such skill. But even as she took his latest inspiration up inside her to the roots, she sternly warned him, "Don't you dare come mooning around my office like a love-struck schoolboy! What do you want my neighbors to think of me? They're sure to gossip if the same man escorts me home more than once in the same month.''

So he asked if she thought it might be safe for him to come around for more legal consultation after harvest time, and she allowed that sounded a tad soon but that she'd risk it, seeing he was able to touch bottom with every stroke whenever she got on top.

Chapter 4

There was much to be said for self-supporting women, but waking a man gentle wasn't one of them. So Longarm found himself out on a deserted Denver street in the cold gray light of dawn with no more than black coffee for breakfast.

He reflected wryly that some might consider that his own fault as he headed over toward the Union Station, walking funny. For Portia had given him his choice of hasty scrambled eggs or more of herself when she'd literally jerked him awake at cock's crow and told him she'd have to hang herself if any of her neighbors spied him leaving after daybreak.

It was way too early to catch any train, if he'd had his saddle and possibles with him. He went to catch some eggs over chili con carne at the all-night beanery next door. The pleasantly plump waitress filled his order and confided she'd be getting off for the day in just a few minutes. Women were like that. Longarm knew that had he been forced to lay over between trains with a raging hard-on a long way from home, she'd have had a boyfriend coming to pick her up after work.

He ordered a slice of mince pie with his third cup of

coffee and left a dime on the counter by his empty plates to show her he didn't think she was too fat. Then he ankled across the Larimer Street bridge to his furnished digs on the less fashionable side of Cherry Creek.

Neither President Rutherford B. nor Miss Lemonade Lucy Hayes were going to know he was in violation of their prissy dress code for government employees whilst he was out in the field in high summer. So he changed into a faded but clean denim riding outfit to separate his well-broken-in cavalry boots from his coffee brown Stetson. He strapped his cross-draw rig around his more comfortable lean hips and filled the pockets of his lighter duds with the usual clutter he packed in the more capacious pockets of his tobacco tweed suit, including the double derringer clipped to one end of his gold-washed watch chain with a plain but accurate timepiece at the other. Having a concealed weapon handy could be as important as knowing for certain what time it might be.

Longarm got down his McClellan army saddle and draped it over the footrail of his seldom-slept-in bed to pack more possibles in the saddlebags. You could carry a heap on a McClellan. Poor old George McClellan had been a failure as a general but one hell of a saddle designer when he'd adapted an Austro-Hungarian cavalry saddle to be issued to the U.S. Army just in time for the War Betwixt the States. It rose higher fore and aft than the English flat saddle, and that open slot running the length of the seat was meant more to cool the horse's spine than to castrate a rider with carelessly loose pants. One of the general's slicker improvements had been studding his new army-issue saddle with brass fittings just right for threading cord or harness straps through. What amounted to a dotted line of such flattened brass loops ran along the leather rim ahead and behind the stirrup leathers. So Longarm always wound up with extra fittings despite all the shit a rider had to carry along when he wasn't certain where he'd be headed or how long it might take.

Seeing it was high summer, the bedroll lashed behind

the cantle had been packed more waterproof than for warmth, with extra cans of grub forming the core of the roll. You seldom needed more than two canteens of water where he'd be riding this time. So he removed a pair. Weather could be tricky up around the North Platte any time of the year. So he added a sheepskin jacket and some woolly chaps to ride under his oilcloth slicker, hoping not to use any of the same but certain it would rain fire, salt, and snowballs if he wasn't ready for 'em.

He packed extra .44-40 rounds for both his six-gun and Winchester '73, chosen with matching loads in mind. He'd scouted for the army often enough to know what a pain in the ass it could be to fumble for a .45 short and wind up with a fist full of .45-70 rifle rounds, albeit, to be fair to the general staff, you sure could hit a man-sized target harder and way farther off with a swamping .45-70.

Longarm preferred more certain shooting at the closer ranges most trouble arose from. He carried his saddle gun in its boot on the off side of his saddle, handy for a right-handed side-draw, with his six-gun balanced higher on his left hip, below the elbow of his rein arm, should any son of a bitch dispute his right of passage.

Once packed, Longarm toted the more awkward than heavy load back across Cherry Creek to the Union Station. Billy Vail had told him to give Deputy Ida Weaver a day's lead on him, and it was way too early to catch the same afternoon Burlington. But Longarm had pals about the railyards and couldn't say how long he'd be tied up along the way with courtesy calls, visits to local newspaper morgues, and such. So he hauled his load through the station and out across the already sun-warmed tracks and gritty ballast to a dispatch shed, to see if he knew anybody on duty there.

He did. One Thumb Thurber, a portly middle-aged cuss whose nickname had fit him since he'd made a mistake with one of those newfangled car couplers, allowed he'd be proud to introduce Longarm to the ca-

27

boose crew of a northbound rattler that would be leaving within the hour for Cheyenne.

As the two of them stepped back out into the morning sunlight, One Thumb felt obliged to warn Longarm, "Be careful what you say when you meet up with the boys. Most of them are all right. But the company's taken on some hard cases to ride the rattlers in warm weather."

Longarm didn't need to ask what One Thumb was talking about. He traveled by rail enough to know a rattler was a string of empty cars being returned or forewarded to some yard in need of the same. Such trains attracted hobos and plain fool kids the way a shaggy dog in need of a bath attracted fleas. So the spoilsports who ran railroads had three choices. They could securely seal each and every empty car, which took heaps of time at both ends when time could add up to money. Or they could tolerate the 'bos in modest numbers, subject to sensible behavior. Or they could hire extra brake bulls to keep them off or throw them off the empties, standing in the yards or rattling across the great outdoors.

Longarm and more easygoing brakemen were inclined to feel sorry for 'bos and tolerate the ones who refrained from crime, vandalism, and shitting inside the rolling stock. Brake bulls hired to crack down on them were recruited amid natural bullies who enjoyed busting heads with baseball bats. Such gents were inclined to forget their manners around others they hadn't been paid to push around. So Longarm told One Thumb he only wanted a ride to Cheyenne, not any discussions about Indian Policy or Professor Darwin.

As they approached the dusty red caboose of the northbound string of empty cars, the dispatcher said the only one your average sane person had to worry about was a towhead they called the Black Swede just the same. Longarm didn't ask why. Assholes named for famously bad tempers didn't interest him, as long as they left him the hell alone. Longarm had never liked bullies to begin with and hadn't been afraid of them since he'd met up with his first one after school, back home in

West-by-God-Virginia. He'd seldom had trouble with the breed since he'd grown up, considerable, with an easy smile and eyes the color of gun muzzles that seldom looked away first.

Nobody had to tell Longarm which of the five railroaders lounging about the caboose was the Black Swede. Aside from being introduced as a Bergman, he stood just under seven feet under his hatless thatch of almost white hair. As One Thumb introduced Longarm all around, it was the Black Swede, rather than the older Irish brakeman, who growled the caboose was already crowded for a dusty run in high summer.

The brakeman, who'd have usually been assumed to be the crewman in charge, shot the Black Swede a thoughtful look but didn't press it. Natural bullies had a sixth sense when it came to knowing just how far they could go with their childish games.

Longarm wasn't up to childish games all the way up to Cheyenne. So he just nodded and said, "He's right. I'd as soon ride lonesome but cooler with this load, up closer to the engine."

Nobody argued. He hadn't expected anyone to demand he crowd in with them. When the Black Swede smirked and asked if he liked to play with himself in the privacy of an empty boxcar, Longarm smiled back just as friendly to reply, "I was hoping you'd suck it for me, seeing you're so interested in another man's dick."

Everybody else laughed. The Black Swede swung down off the steps of the caboose to stand face to face with Longarm, staring down at the tall deputy for a change as he demanded, "Did I just hear somebody call me a cocksucker, little darling?"

Longarm went on smiling up at him as he replied, "I thought I just heard you make such an offer. Mayhaps it would be best if you'd just refrain from any and all suggestions about my cock if you ain't really interested in it."

The Black Swede said, "I ain't interested in anything

but your big mouth, passenger boy! Didn't your momma never tell you a man could get himself killed by shooting off his mouth around grown men?''

Longarm quietly replied, ''You mention my mother one more time and you're the one who'll wind up deader than last summer's cow shit!''

Before the Black Swede could say anything else to make Longarm's eyes grow even colder, One Thumb snapped, ''Swede, you're talking to a man packing three guns and a rep for sincerety. Why don't all of you boys get aboard this damn rattler, wherever you want to ride her, so we can send her on her damn way?''

Longarm picked up his awkward load, braced the saddle tree against his left hip to leave his gun hand free, and headed north toward the engine with no further comment.

One Thumb tagged along, saying something about handing orders up to the engine crew. But as soon as they were out of earshot, he muttered, ''Jesus H. Christ, Longarm. I asked you to watch your manners around the Black Swede and you called him a cocksucker!''

Longarm shrugged and trudged on as he replied, ''I was trying to be polite. You don't talk nice to a man who's just called you a jerk-off. If you let him get away with that, he'll call you something worse, and if you let him get away with that, he'll throw your hat up on the roof.''

One Thumb said, ''The Black Swede's outgrown that stage. The company don't allow it. But he still packs a Harrington and Richardson double-action belly gun. He's inclined to use it, too. We got him off the Kansas and Missouri, cheap, after he'd shot two 'bos in self-defense, or so he says.''

They were passing the open doorway of a boxcar dunnaged with a carpet of clean hay. It smelled as if they'd been shipping kegs of rum. Longarm tossed his heavily laden saddle aboard as he assured the dispatcher he meant to stray nowhere near that caboose or the surly brake bull. So One Thumb wished him luck and went on up to jaw with the engine crew.

Longarm moved his saddle back from the doorway and cleared a space of bare flooring so's it would be safe to smoke a mite as he lounged with one elbow in the saddle. He didn't light up just yet. He had a long ride ahead with a limited quantity of tobacco. He fished some of the carbon copies old Henry at the office had let him have on the little anyone really knew about those Wyoming wildwomen. He'd read through the lot of them already. But he read through them some more as long as he had the time and no draft was fluttering the onionskin paper. By the time the train started up with a plaintive whistle and a rude jerk, he'd decided once again that Billy Vail was sending him on a snipe hunt. He found it tough to believe local, county, and territorial lawmen were party to some fiendish female secret society's evil plot to take over the West. The trouble with vast conspiracies by government officials was that nobody in charge of a whole government *needed* to behave so sneaky. Men in positions of power had no more call to hide the fact they were running things than a cattle baron or mining magnate had to deny he was rich. El Presidente Diaz down Mexico didn't need to plot against the folk he ruled. He just told them to jump, and if they didn't ask how high, he sent his *rurales* to shove 'em up against a handy wall and shoot them.

Of course, he told himself, Uncle John Chisum had tried to pretend he had no hand in the series of back shootings remembered as the Lincoln County War. But he hadn't fooled anybody and, greedy as the Santa Fe Ring had been, they hadn't asked New Mexico lawmen to deny a thing was going on down yonder. Lawmen could be bought. It happened all the time. But it cost serious money, and nobody did it without some serious reasons of their own in mind.

"Cherchez la motif!" Longarm tried for, wondering if he had that right from the little French he'd studied in bed with a Métis he sure remembered fondly. He

knew that whether he'd pronounced that right or not, neither he nor any other poor but honest lawman was going to be able to come to grips with little more than a slippery bait-can of disturbing womanly whims. To catch anybody really up to no good, he had to decide what in blue thunder they were up to!

Cheyenne lay a hundred miles north of Denver by crow. It took a few extra miles of bends in the railroad right of way as the tracks wound around the higher swells of the rolling prairie in the rain shadow of the Front Range. A low-balling empty rattler naturally took way longer than a passenger varnish or even a high-balling freight. But Longarm wasn't upset when they pulled off the main line near Fort Collins to let a more serious train thunder past. He knew that poky or not, he'd get to Cheyenne around noon. That would give him plenty of time for the courtesy call Billy Vail expected him to make at the Cheyenne federal building and still catch the shortline combination up to the North Platte Country. So he was just lounging there on the hay, smoking a cheroot as he leaned against his saddle, gazing out the open doorway at nothing much but rolling grass, when all of a sudden this dirty-faced kid wearing raggedy boy's jeans and long blond pigtails rolled over the sill to almost land on top of him, just as the train was starting up again.

As she hovered above Longarm on her hands and knees, the dirty-faced but sort of pretty kid gasped, "Oh, I thought this car would be empty!"

To which Longarm could only reply, "It ain't. Where might you be headed in such a hurry, sis?"

She gulped and stammered, "Keller's Crossing on the high plains of Wyoming Territory. Please don't hurt me, mister. I'll fuck you if I have to. But you don't have to hurt me to have your way with me, and I purely wish you wouldn't!"

Chapter 5

Her name was Daisy Gunn and she claimed to be seventeen. It was tougher to judge such matters when a gal was wearing mannish duds too big for her. By the time they'd established this much, Longarm had broken out a can of pork and beans and opened it with his pocketknife. From the way the barefoot waif wolfed down his trail grub, he surmised she hadn't been eating regular of late. He opened a can of tomato preserves for her to wash down the beans and cut the greasy aftertaste of the same before he took to questioning her serious.

So they were rolling along at a merry clip, with the one opening to the shady side, as he heard her sad but hardly unfamiliar story. There was something about the sound of a railroad whistle in the night to inspire young folk stuck with a heap of chores on a hardscrabble homestead to try their luck hopping freight trains to far places. She said, so far, she'd seen eleven states and been raped fourteen times by 'bos and bulls she'd found herself traveling with. She shyly confessed she'd been scared skinny by the sheer size of Longarm when she'd suddenly found herself in his company with the car already in motion. She said she'd saved her virtue one time by

rolling off a moving train and decided never to do anything that painful again. For she was getting used to
getting raped, while an ass-over-teakettle roll down a
railroad bank could tear up a gal and her duds considerable.

Longarm lit a fresh cheroot without offering her one,
seeing she seemed a mite young for such bad habits, and
told her, "This rattler won't take neither of us any farther than the Cheyenne yards. You'll need to grab a ride
aboard a feeder line out of Cheyenne and you'll likely
have to ride the rods because they hardly ever send empties on to any such spur heads. You were going to tell
me how come you're headed for Keller's Crossing via
boxcar, weren't you?"

Daisy said, "Another girl in Pueblo told me women
have the same rights as men up Wyoming way and that
this girls' club is running the whole show in that township. Everywhere else I go, looking for work or just a
place to flop, some mean old man takes advantage of
me, and I'm getting mighty sick and tired of being
slapped around and raped by mean old men."

Longarm allowed he'd heard they had gals voting and
holding public office up Wyoming way. Then he casually asked if she recalled the name of that other gal
who'd told her of such wonders.

It didn't work. Daisy shrugged and said, "I don't recall if she said we should call her Babs or Belle when
they were holding us all in that jail. Her pimp came to
bail her out around three in the morning. I wound up
getting thirty days for vag, making mattress covers and
getting passed back and forth by two older lizzy gals. I
reckon I'd still be there if this dirty old man hadn't come
by to pick out a prisoner of his choosing. He said he'd
paid my fine and so I'd have to pay him off in trade,
three ways for three dollars. If you ask me, he only
bribed one of the turnkeys because my thirty days were
almost up, and I don't think it was fair that I had to
spend almost a week in a stuffy loft with that dirty old
man before he'd let me go."

Longarm made a mental note that Wyoming might not be the only place some peace officers seemed to be abusing their authority. But since you could only eat an apple one bite at a time he told her, "I might have another business proposition for you, Miss Daisy, seeing we're both headed the same way."

She sat up, cross-legged, to smile down uncertainly at his relaxed form as she replied, "Well, all right. You ain't bad looking, and I've learned to sort of like it when a man ain't cruel or ugly."

He smiled dryly up at her to declare, "That wasn't the proposition I had in mind, no offense. For you to understand just what I want, I'm going to have to tell you more about myself and my reasons for going on up to the same country you're headed for."

He left out a lot, of course, as he explained he was a federal lawman investigating the very situation that seemed to have inspired her own enthusiasm for such a feminist utopia.

He said, "You have my word I ain't looking to get any innocent ladies in trouble, Miss Daisy. We've had what we call conflicting reports in my line of work. You'll doubtless be pleased to learn that some other federal lawmen have reported favorsome on a cattle country community where women hold much the same political powers as their menfolk."

She nodded and said, "That's what I heard in that holding pen. As soon as I get there I mean to search for work, and dast any dirty old man declare I have to fuck him first, I mean to have the law on him!"

Longarm said that sounded reasonable as he tried to decide how he wanted to word his own job offer. Heaps of ladies he admired had a cunt hair crosswise over this womens-suffering bullshit, and a man had to watch his step lest he put a foot in his mouth whilst saying word one on the subject.

Longarm considered himself fair-minded, and he'd often told the sweet little things it was no skin off his nose if women got the same pay for the same work, got to vote, the same as any male drunk, or got on top in bed, if that was their pleasure. But the gals who took this suffering bullshit serious could be proddy about it as a Holy Roller asked to comment on Professor Darwin, and you had to keep assuring all concerned you weren't in league with the forces of evil, even whilst you were trying to agree with them.

He was about to make mention of her unshod and unkempt state when their casual view of rolling range to the east was largely blocked by the Black Swede, swinging down from the rolling car's roof like a big blonde ape.

The brake bull handled himself well aboard a moving train. After gracefully running nearly the length of the rattler along the catwalks up above, he kipped his considerable bulk in through the open doorway to land astride Longarm's stretched-out boots as he grinned down at the two of them like a shit-eating dog to growl, "Well, well, what have we here, a famous lawman too proud to jerk off and a sissy 'bo fixing to do it for him or . . . Bless my stars, is that a gal you've been hogging to yourself up here, Long dong?"

Daisy seemed to shrink down beside him like one of the wildflowers she was named for, caught in the glare of a desert sun. But Longarm didn't even sound as testy as he felt when he calmly replied, "Watch your mouth. Miss Daisy, here, is with me, Bergman."

The Black Swede looming over them said, "So I see. We don't have to share the pretty little thing with the rest of the crew, as long as you're willing to share her with me."

Longarm grimaced and quietly said, "Hang some crepe on your nose in memory of the dead brain inside. We'll be rolling into Cheyenne soon enough, and I'm sure you have plenty of sweethearts along Crow Creek. I told you this young lady is with me. But if it's any comfort to you, she ain't with me that way, and there's nothing you'd be interested in to share."

The Black Swede was suddenly looming over them

with a snub-nosed nickel-plated six-gun in hand as he said, "That tears it. I've had all of your smart mouth I can stand, and now you're fixing to get off my damned train and walk the rest of the way!"

Longarm shifted his weight some to stare thoughtfully through the spread legs of the bully at the passing scenery, observing, "We're doing better than twenty miles an hour right now, Bergman."

The Black Swede laughed with as much warmth as your average fox in a henhouse and declared, "I've seen men jump off a train doing forty and *still* the rascals lived. You aim to jump off like a man or have me toss you off like a sack of dead shit? I ain't bluffing. Go for that .44-40 you're half laying across, if you doubt my word I'm willing and able to gun any son of a bitch who crosses me!"

Longarm tried, "The rest of the crew saw me climb aboard this train, with the permit of your dispatcher, Bergman."

The Black Swede proved how well he deserved his ominous nickname when he just shrugged and said, "I ain't worried about them. I just told you nobody crosses me if they know what's good for them. Are you going to do as I say or do I have to waste a bullet on your thick skull?"

Then the Black Swede gave a sudden wild yelp, managed to fire one wild shot up into the car's roofing, and appeared to vanish into thin air with a mournful wail.

Daisy Gunn sat bolt upright, staring wide-eyed out the gaping doorway as she asked, "How did you do that, Custis? Are you some sort of magician?"

Longarm rolled up to his feet and moved over to the doorway to lean out and peer back down the right of way, where a mighty dusty but still conscious form was trying to get back up from the summer-killed grass without much luck.

Longarm rejoined the girl and sat back down beside her, saying, "Aw, he hurt his little leg. Might have been the fall. Might have been my kicking him in the kneecap like so. It wasn't magic, Miss Daisy. This other lady who taught me that particular trick called it Jewish Gypsy. It's a style of wrestling they invented over in Japan one time, and this Texas gal in the import-export business learned some from her Japanese hired help. I forget what they call the Jewish Gypsy trick I used just now. But like he pointed out, it would have been dumb to go for my six-gun or derringer with him standing over us point-blank. But I'd already noticed he was astride one of my boots stretched out in the hay, and I saw he was shifting his weight from one of his own legs to the other as the deck swayed under us. So I timed to when I should twist my right ankle to hook my toes behind his left heel, and next time he had his weight on that leg with the knee locked, I only had to kick the cap of said knee with my other boot to send him out the doorway backward.''

She marveled, "You surely did. I wish I knew some of them Jewish Gypsy tricks. They'd surely come in handy, riding the rails.''

Longarm remembered the cheroot he'd been gripping unsmoked between his teeth and enjoyed a luxurious drag before he told her, "We were talking about your future as a feminist up Wyoming way before we were so rudely interrupted. We'll be getting into the Cheyenne yards within the hour. Whether anyone else on board watched that brake bull learning to fly backward or not, I don't want anyone to see us getting off together. So we'd best drop off just outside the yards.''

She pouted. "Aw, I ain't that disgusting to be seen with. Some say I ain't half bad to look at, bare ass, after a warm bath.''

Longarm said, "I mean to sneak you into the Pilgrim Hotel and let you enjoy a nice long soak whilst I rustle you up more ladylike duds and run some other errands. I have to pay a courtesy call, over to the federal building, and then, if they'll let me, I'd like to browse a mite through the newspaper morgue at the *Wyoming Eagle*. After that we'll be on our way. Whilst you're riding with me I can likely get them to pay you four bits a day and found. How do you like it so far?"

She clapped her grimy hands and declared, "I like it a heap and you won't be sorry. I'll wash myself good, inside and out, and you can do it to me any way but Greek, if I'm half right about how a man your size has to be hung."

Longarm sighed and said, "I don't want to bugger you, and if I did I wouldn't. The deal I have in mind calls for you remaining as pure as the driven snow."

She flared, "What's wrong with me, you stuck-up thing? We've both agreed I could use a bath and these men's duds I stole off a clothesline may not do my girl-ish figure justice. But heaps of men have told me I look swell with no duds on at all. Would you like me to strip and show you?"

Longarm laughed and said, "Hold the thought for now. I can see how pretty you are, and I ain't no sissy when it comes to pretty gals. But I'm a lawman, on a mission, and I want to hire you to help me carry it out, see?"

She didn't. She said she'd be proud to help him out any way but Greek, any time he said the word.

He said, "Pay attention and you have my permit to help yourself out in that hot tub whilst I pay attention to them other chores I mentioned. I can't let you play that way with me, or vice versa, because with any luck I may wind up calling you as a disinterested federal witness, and you can't swear you ain't interested if the other side can accuse you of having enjoyed any slap and tickle with the arresting officer."

She asked who on earth he wanted her to bear witness against in any fool federal court.

He answered, simply, "If I knew that now, I wouldn't need your help. Somebody where we're headed may or may not be abusing his or her authority. If that ain't it, we'll still have to seek an injunction against sheer stupidity before some poor nester gal or schoolmarm is killed in a line of duty she was never meant for. We'll have heaps of time to talk about it later. Right now I can see by the truck farms we're passing that we're coming into Cheyenne. We ought to be slowing down for the trestle over Crow Creek and the yards beyond, ere long.''

He rolled to his knees to slide his McClellan and possibles way closer to the open doorway as he told her, ''I'll tell you when to follow me, tight, as I roll out just before we enter the yards. This car won't be moving more than eight or ten miles an hour by then, and you did say you'd had some experience in these matters, right?''

She allowed she could teach him a thing or two about hopping on or off fool freight cars. Then she asked to hear more about this offer of a job that paid so well but didn't require her to pleasure him.

Longarm smiled wolfishly and said, ''Oh, I'll be pleased as punch with you if we can sneak you as far as Keller's Crossing without a Wyoming soul knowing you're really riding with me. You do know how to ride a horse good, don't you? I can't see any other way for the two of us to drift into Keller's Crossing in cahoots but not climbing down off the same train. The spur rails and the old Overland Trail both follow that stretch of the North Platte. But most everybody in your average trail town turns out whenever a train or coach rolls in.''

Daisy said she'd noticed that and asked, once more, for more details about the particular chores he had in mind for her, if none of them seemed to involve them even smiling at each other in public.

He said they had to be thinking of getting off, now, as they rolled across the Crow Creek trestle. He wasn't sure just how he ought to tell a determined shemale sufferer how he might have to ask her to help him fuck some other members of her sisterhood.

Chapter 6

A barefoot blonde wearing pants and pigtails seemed to attract odd looks as she tagged after Longarm and his saddle through the outskirts of Cheyenne. So when they stopped for some soda pop and directions at a neighborhood general store, Longarm bought Daisy a straw plowboy's hat and told her to shove her braids up inside the crown for now, in the hopes she might be taken for a raggedy farm youth instead of a gal dressed scandalous.

The Pilgrim Hotel near the U.P. Depot, like most good saloons or hotels, had discreet side entrances for social delicacies such as a man wanting to smuggle a gal in for a drink or whatever without the whole world having to know about it.

So Longarm had Daisy roost on a hitching rail by the hotel stable entrance while he and the McClellan went into the lobby to hire adjoining rooms up on the second floor. He signed himself in as who he was and told them he was expecting another government agent to arrive later in the day. He signed Daisy in as D. G. Crawford and never said word one about her gender. He pocketed both keys and said he'd store his own baggage topside before he went to see what was holding old D. G. The musty-haired old room clerk didn't seem to care one way or the other. Hotels only worried about baggage or just how many might be upstairs when they suspected they might be stiffed on the going room rates.

Leaving the McClellan in the room he'd hired for his own use, he went out through the stable exit to fetch the barefoot Daisy. He led her in and up the back stairs as he explained why she was signed in as somebody else. He said, "It's more important for me to remember your fake name because folk are less likely to ask you who I've been expecting aboard the afternoon train from Denver. I like to use the name, Crawford, because it's easy for me to recall. Crawford Long, the doc who invented painless surgery, was a hero to a heap of us during the war, and I've always hoped we might be kin. After that I know a reporter Crawford on the *Denver Post* who lies about me all the time, and I figure one good turn deserves another. I think Crawford is a Scotch name, like Gunn, anyways."

She asked him who he was calling Scotch. He told her he'd known a Scotchman named Gunn one time and added, "Came from a part of Scotland they call Sutherland because it's as far north as Scotland goes. I've yet to fathom why Scotchmen wear skirts and like oatmeal, either. How come you didn't know your name was Scotch? I've yet to meet anybody with a Scotch name who didn't know it was Scotch."

She didn't answer as they entered the room he'd hired for her near the head of the back stairs. Before she could come up with a lie, Longarm told her, "I might of known today ain't the first occasion a runaway by any name might have had occasion to change her name. Don't confound me with any other names, true or false. Just remember you're the one and original D. G. Crawford until further notice."

He opened the door to the bath her room shared with his own. He told her, "Both doors bolt on the inside lest two hotel guests who don't know each other meet buck-naked in here. I want you to keep your hall door bolted. I'll hang one of them don't-disturbs on it, and none of the hotel help have any call to come in here before we check out, official, in twenty-four hours.''

She looked unsettled as she asked him where he was going without her. So Longarm said, "I told you I had some chores to tend here in the territorial capital. I'll bring you back some more ladylike duds to wear as we wend our way on to Keller's Crossing. What are your favorite colors, Miss Daisy?''

She said yellow and blue.

He said he'd try to match the colors of her hair and eyes when he shopped for her. He added, "I'll bring us some warm grub whilst I'm at it. I dasn't take you out to supper because I don't want anybody to know we're together. Keep your door bolted and don't answer if anybody knocks, in spite of the don't-disturb. It won't be me because I'm booked in next door. I'll let my ownself in or out through the don't-disturb on my door with my key. I'll come back to you by way of this bath. So don't bolt *that* door after you finish scrubbing behind both ears.''

They both smiled at that picture. But then she allowed she felt scared as well as totally at sea about all this mysterious shit, as she put it.

He took out his double derringer and unhooked it from his watch chain as he told her he'd explain the whole deal before he'd call on her to do anything but stay put. He asked if she knew how to use a gun. When she said she did, he wasn't surprised.

He handed her the derringer and said, "Don't use this unless you have to. I'll be switched with snakes if I can see why you might have to, but, like Ben Franklin said about death and taxes, nothing else in this old world is certain. Just make certain it ain't a nosy maid or a drunk at the wrong room door before you let fly.''

As she gingerly took the bitty pistol, Longarm hauled out his wallet and produced a ten-dollar paper certificate. She stared at it goggle-eyed as he held it out to her, explaining, "If I ain't back by checkout time, you'll know I ain't coming back and you're on your own. I can't spare more. But a gal with a gun and a week's wages ought to get way farther than she might without 'em."

The dirty-faced waif almost sobbed, "What are you talking about? Why do you say you might not be back? Who's after you? Who's after either one of us, Custis?"

Longarm smiled down reassuringly and told her, "Nobody is after *you,* unless you've been hiding more than your real name from me. I don't know as anybody in particular is after me. But a man picks up enemies riding six or eight years for the Justice Department. You were there when that surly brake bull started up with me. I reckon there's something about my rep or the way I walk that inspires the mean and restless to start up with me. I've never liked them all that much, and I reckon they sense it some way. Like wild critters can tell when you're drawing a bead on 'em."

He didn't have the time or inclination to go into the times a crook with something to hide had seen fit to set up an ambush for the lawman probing into his or her shady doings. If there was some master plan behind those Wyoming wildwomen, neither local, territorial, nor federal lawmen from the Cheyenne District Court had been able to detect it. Gunning the first outside lawmen sent to poke around would be sort of dumb for a mastermind.

He had no call to tell a white gal how to run a bath or use the hotel soap and towels. So he just asked her to save one towel for him to use later, then let himself out the far door between the tub and commode.

He picked up another don't-disturb in the room he'd signed himself into, ducked out in the hall, and locked up before he hung both the don't-disturbs on their adjoining hall knobs. He made certain nobody was anywhere about before he dropped to one knee and wedged a match stem in the crack of his locked door, under the

44

bottom hinge, because an inside bolt was one thing, but a latch key was easy to duplicate.

Then he eased down the back steps and out by way of the stable to the sunny street.

He'd gone two city blocks before a hall porter on a landing he'd avoided asked an upstairs maid, "What's going on in two hundred eight and nine? They both have don't-disturbs out and it's barely afternoon."

The maid smiled dirty and confided, "Nobody's asleep in either room. I was just coming from a checkout down the hall when that one who says he's a lawman snuck his pretty boy up the back stairs."

The hall porter blinked and demanded, "Are you sure it was a *boy*? I've heard heaps of things about the famous Longarm, but this is the first I've ever heard of him queering young boys!"

The maid, a plain woman who might have felt left out, shrugged and said, "Have your own way. It was a *girl* with dirty bare feet, ragged jeans, work shirt, and straw hat. Those trash whites down along Crow Creek have adopted a new fashion. They've taken to wearing men's duds to make themselves more tempting."

The hall porter laughed, dirty, and decided, "Wait till I tell the boys the famous Longarm is a queer! I mean, I always had my doubts about Wild Bill's shoulder-length curly locks, but who'd have ever thought a gunslick with Longarm's rep as a lady's man would shack up with young boys for Gawd's sake!"

The lady's man they were gossiping about made it to the Cheyenne Federal Building before they were done with him. Once inside he found that the cuss who'd declared virtue was its own reward had never had to argue Federal Jurisdiction with Billy Vail's thoroughly pissed-off opposite number in Wyoming Territory.

The somewhat younger and leaner but just as crusty U.S. Marshal Winslow Morris, formerly of the Iowa Volunteers and mighty stuck up about that, too, told Longarm he was the victim of a cruel practical joke or riding for blithering assholes. Gritting his big yellow teeth on his own version of an expensive cigar in an oak-paneled office of his own, Marshal Morris insisted he's had his own deputies look into the rash of arrest warrants breaking out in Keller's Crossing. He said they'd gone over the township's voter registration and financial ledgers while they were at it.

Longarm, seated in a guest chair made out of elk antlers in this case, nodded soberly and said, "I've read your own reports. More than once. Anyone can see nothing cruel or unusual seems to be going on up here in Wyoming Territory, sir. Those lovely young things your lady J.P. keeps arming with dead-or-alive warrants have been gunning men down in other parts. As far south as Texas and as far east as Missouri. We make it eight such men, so far. Shot down like dogs without even the pretence of due process."

Marshal Morris grimaced and said, "I told Simp Glover it looked a mite neater when a deputy throwed a suspect's hat across an alley and ordered him to run and fetch it before he fired. But old Simp says—"

"Simp?" Longarm cut in, demanding, "Might we be talking about the county he-sheriff up yonder, name of Glover, now that I think back to my own notes?"

Marshal Morris nodded and replied, "We are. Simp's a good old boy with a herd of nigh two thousand head grazing alongside the North Platte. They elected him county sheriff because he scouted for the cav during Red Cloud's War north of Fort Laramie and kept his hair when all about him were losing their own. Like I said, I told Simp we were catching Ned from other parts when his shemale deputies got past three killings in one season. Simp says he never told nobody to shoot nobody, male or shemale. I told you he had to be *elected* up yonder, and Keller's Crossing is named after old Dutch Keller, founder of the considerable Keller cattle clan in them parts."

Longarm nodded soberly and said, "I was wondering how Edith Penn Keller of Keller's Crossing got appointed justice of the peace. What can you tell me about

46

Rita Mae Reynolds, appointed undersheriff for her township by the doubtless grateful Sheriff Glover?''

Marshal Morris shifted the stogie between his bared teeth and told Longarm, ''A heap of Keller's Crossing residents who ain't named Keller seem to be named Reynolds. I know what you're thinking. It's still the way things work in tight-knit rural townships. Boss Tweed took care of his kith and kin in New York City, and Boss Buckley is still taking care of his kith and kin out Frisco way. Neither you, me, nor nobody can reform such setups until and unless somebody in the catbird seat really fucks up.''

''What do you call deputizing young gals and sending them clean out of the territory to shoot folk?'' Longarm soberly demanded.

Morris shrugged and replied in an easy tone, ''Good riddance? We ain't talking about young gals shooting *folk*! Every man jack of them eight wants was an outlaw with a rep who'd made the mistake of armed robbery in or about Keller's Crossing!''

''How come?'' asked Longarm, mildly pointing out, ''There's hardly anything up yonder but a bitty trail town surrounded by miles of open range. As far as I've been able to see from the onion skin reports I was issued, ain't one case of *stock theft* been reported. All eight of those dead outlaws were accused of taking cash and valuables at gunpoint.''

Morris nodded, saying, ''I read the same crime statistics. Keller's Crossing sits at the junctions of east-west and north-south trails. It serves as both a handy river ford and the best layover for travelers switching betwixt stagecoach and rail.''

''Like a spider in the middle of its web?'' asked Longarm dryly.

Morris shrugged and answered simply, ''I suspect Dutch Keller had more honest profits in mind when he staked out his claims along the North Platte just south of what was then pure Sioux Country. In any case, there the town sits, and outlaws will fly in and out of the web for fun and profit. Undersheriff Reynolds, being a gal, herself, may favor gal deputies more than you or me might. Our own judges already warned Justice Keller not to put down dead-or-alive on those arrest warrants anymore.''

''You mean she still gets to issue the dumb writs?'' Longarm asked.

Morris said, ''Sure she does. We told her she only has the power to order a suspect arrested and hauled in to be remanded to higher county authorities. Said authorities agree things might have gotten a mite out of hand. But, meanwhile, Undersheriff Rita Mae had the same right as any other peace officer to deputize pro tem under the old common law of *posse comitatus.*''

Longarm grimaced and said, ''*Posse comitatus* is one thing, and sweet young things executing criminals without a trial is another. Leaving aside the rights or wrongs under common law, what sort of paid-up peace officer would deputize an armed and dangerous young gal to . . . Son of a stupid cotton-picking bitch!''

''I hope you ain't talking about me,'' Marshal Morris said quietly.

Longarm sighed and said, ''Nope. Talking about me! It's so easy to point out the mistakes of others until you catch your fool self in the very same mistakes!''

Morris asked, ''Are you saying you've been deputizing and arming young gals, old son?''

To which Longarm was forced to reply, ''Only one. So far. But a man can sure feel foolish when he looks in the mirror to see egg on his own face!''

Chapter 7

Longarm was grateful for his sensible denim jacket and open shirt collar as he trudged down Central Avenue with his brain chasing its own tail.

It was a typical summer afternoon on the high plains, with the thin air conspiring with the naked sun in a cloudless cobalt blue sky to surprise folk. It felt like someone had just opened a furnace door whenever he crossed a sunlit patch of plank walk or mummy-dust side street, but it was pleasantly cool in any shade, thanks to the way a body got to sweat so dry at this altitude.

His thoughts were in more of a whirl as he considered how easy, and how innocent, it might be for an under-sheriff more sissy than his ownself to come up with the notion of recruiting a woman to aid and abet the law. It *was* easier for an innocent-looking gal to pussyfoot up to a suspect and ask questions, or pull triggers, than it might be for the least ferocious-looking boy. Since word had gone 'round about that harmless-looking Kid Antrim, Billy the Kid, or whatever the little shit was calling himself lately, a halfway-sober gunslick tended to think twice before he let down his guard in the company of a skinny little runt he didn't know right well. But gents who didn't grin like shit-eating dogs at pretty gals were seldom found along the Owlhoot Trail to begin with.

He'd decided to just send Daisy on her way and proceed the usual way as he mounted the steps of the Western Union office near the depot.

But as he was block-lettering the telegram form to Billy Vail, he pictured how she was going to take it when he just told her to go hop another freight train. He'd told her she had a job at four bits a day, however temporary. After that he still couldn't see how the hell farm girls or shop clerks in the full flush of youth as well as skirts went about tracking down experienced owlhoot riders.

He explained about Daisy Gunn and his future plans for her as he lettered on. He had to send this already windy field report at nickel a word flat rates if he expected his home office to get it before it was too late in the day to matter. So he didn't waste nickels asking them to see if there were any wants out on little Daisy Gunn. He knew Henry would get cracking in the file room before Billy ordered him to scout her good.

He told them where he'd be that afternoon and which train they meant to catch to Fort Laramie after dark. Then he told the telegraph clerk to reverse the charges, and he left Western Union with a less troubled mind, humming the words to that old church song he often recalled at such times. It went,

"Farther along, we'll know more about it.
Farther along, we'll understand why.
Cheer up, my brothers, walk in the sunshine.
We'll understand it,
All by and by."

"There's got to be some iron-fisted man behind that velvet glove handing out cheap badges and childish arrest warrants," he decided, in spite of the advice he'd just given himself. It was all right, if not downright smart, for a lawman to keep changing his mind as he stepped through the sunlight and shadow of a mysterious world. Men in any line who made up their minds before all the cards had been dealt were most likely to get up from the table broke.

He came upon a lady's notions shop a block farther along and ducked inside to see about some decent duds for his raggedy recruit at the hotel. A little old lady with hair the color of a barbed-wire coil and an ass that wasn't half bad said she'd be proud to rustle him up a blue and yellow print frock if he'd tell her the size of his young lady.

Longarm squinted thoughtfully down at the little old lady in a manner to bring some color to her dear old cheeks as he decided, "She's about your height, but not built quite as curvacious, ma'am. I reckon any pretty frock you could fit your own fine figure in would be safe for her to slip into."

The little old lady laughed in a surprisingly young tone and got some frocks to choose between from out back. Longarm could see at a glance how nice one print featuring yellow asters on a robin's-egg-blue background would offset Daisy's coloring. So he allowed he'd take it and added the gal might be able to use a travel duster to wear over her finery.

Finding an ankle-length tan poplin duster in the right size was easier. The elderly but nicely put-together shop lady balked when he asked her to hoist her skirts and throw one foot up on the counter.

She asked him what on earth he thought she was selling, and Longarm almost blushed, his ownself, as he explained he had to pick out some shoes and socks for that other lady.

The one he was talking to asked if he couldn't check the size of the shoes his young lady was already wearing.

He didn't want to explain checking into the Pilgrim with a raggedy barefoot waif, so he allowed it was supposed to be a birthday surprise.

That worked. The little old lady lined up a whole mess

of high-button shoes on the counter for him to make an educated guess. He squinted his eyes to picture bare feet on that hotel rug and decided, "I might be able to guess smarter if you were to show me riding boots, instead, ma'am. I'm used to taking army showers with bare feet of all shapes and sizes. But I picture the same in boots instead of fine footwear."

The little old lady pursed her lips and declared, "Riding boots, with a calico print? Well, you did say you wanted to surprise her!"

Longarm chuckled at the picture and replied, "Matter of fact, we may go riding, later. You'd best throw in a summerweight riding habit. Split skirts, if you have 'em. I've never seen the lady ride, and some younger gals have taken to riding astride of late, out this way."

The older woman sniffed, said she'd noticed, and Longarm wasn't sure whether she was feeling shocked or left out as she rummaged in the back some more to produce a whipcord bolero jacket and split calf-length skirt she allowed would fit anyone who could get into that dress and duster.

Longarm bought a frilly blouse and a silly gal's hat to go with the other purchases. He figured Daisy could wear that more mannish straw hat with her riding habit. When he paid off he was glad he'd told Billy Vail about hiring Daisy for four bits and found. Dressing her up civilized had used up some pocket jingle!

As he thanked the nice old lady and stepped back outside it came to him that Daisy was waiting, in her bath or wrapped in a towel, with nothing in the way of underwear if he was any judge of a gal's hind end in raggedy jeans. But he was out to make her presentable in public, not to fill her damned hope chest, and he was fixing to catch holy ned as it was when he charged that silly summer hat to the U.S. government.

But even as he stepped down off the walk to cross the dusty sunlit street, he could picture the gallant little smile of a gal putting on a spanking new dress over bare flesh. So he muttered, "Shit!" and spun on one heel to retrace his steps to that shop.

So the bullet aimed at him with his next step out of the shade missed the small of his back by a whisker to hum on up Central Avenue until it thunked into the rump of a tethered cow pony and caused considerable excitement out front of that one saloon.

As the rump-shot pony neighed and bucked loose up yonder, Longarm threw his package over a watering trough and followed it headfirst to land on one shoulder and roll across the plank walk behind a rain barrel as, sure enough, a second bullet thunked into said barrel and Longarm pegged a shot of his own at a haze of gunsmoke drifting up from behind the false front of a shop across the avenue.

The little old lady popped out of her doorway like she thought it was the front of a cuckoo clock, demanding to know what was going on.

Longarm yelled, "Get back inside before you get your ass shot off!"

So she did and then a million years went by as rainwater pissed out of the barrel he lay behind to run across the planks and water the dry dust and horse turds with nothing else moving for blocks until Longarm heard a voice from behind him calling, "I see you behind yon rain barrel, cowboy! Rise and shine with your hands polite if you don't want two rounds of number nine buck up your ass. For I am the law and I have the drop on you!"

Longarm rolled on one elbow to gaze back along the shady side of the avenue. He called out to the older jasper aiming a double-barrel Greener his way, "I'm the law my ownself. Federal. Watch out for the false front above the stationery store catty-corner across from me. I suspect it was a Henry or Winchester that just fired my way, twice. That pony running off from the saloon behind you would have gone down if it had been hit with a buffalo round."

The Cheyenne lawman eased along the walk toward

Longarm with his Greener trained more politely, albeit no shotgun charges were about to hurt anybody sheltered behind plank siding, that far off.

But the old-timer wasn't dumb. As he joined Longarm behind that big barrel, a lesser light tagging after him asked what came next. So the Cheyenne lawman said, "Go back. Get Pete and Simmons to go with you as you circle wide to move in behind that stationery store. Some son of a bitch just shot Jeff Wolheim's pony from yonder rooftop, and if he's still there I want him dead or alive!"

As his backup moved off, the old-timer introduced himself as a Marshal Casey. Town marshals got to do that. They both knew Longarm was the senior peace officer present when he introduced himself as a deputy marshal. He'd already told Casey he was federal.

Casey naturally wanted to know what the hell the two of them were doing behind that barrel.

Longarm told him, "I was only passing through on my way to a trail town called Keller's Crossing. I had just sent a wire saying I suspected I was on a fool's errand. You just pointed out how easy it is to say dead or alive in the heat of the moment. But somebody seems intent on keeping me from getting any closer to his or her odd situation."

Marshal Casey asked if they were talking about that rash of dead outlaws occasioned by tomboys packing guns and badges, by the great horned spoon.

Longarm said the attorney general and Billy Vail were sort of shocked by such unladylike behavior as well and asked what a lawman closer to the scene might have heard about it.

Casey hunkered around to brace his back against the planking with his shotgun across his knees as he replied, "You name it. We've heard it. None of them crazy shootouts have transpired here in the territory. But the smart-money boys have passed the word it ain't too smart to go anywhere's near Keller's Crossing with a running iron in one's saddle or larceny on one's mind."

Longarm cocked a thoughtful brow and said, "Ain't had any reports about lost, strayed, or stolen cows. But you just now said you've been hearing all sorts of rumors. Reminds me of other trail towns I've run across. There's nothing like tales of blood and slaughter to keep the faint at heart at bay, or, contrariwise, attract trouble the way an open pot of honey attracts flies."

Marshal Casey said, "Most of the saddle tramps and mean drunks in these parts would seem to have been avoiding Keller's Crossing since them loco lady peace officers have taken to acting so hard-hearted."

Longarm nodded grimly and replied, "I just said that. A heap of naturally wild kids settled down once word got around that Dodge City was a piss-poor place to shoot out streetlamps. On the other hand, hard cases such as Clay Allison, John Wesley Hardin, and those murderous Thompson brothers might never have drifted into Dodge if it hadn't sounded so lively."

Marshal Casey nodded thoughtfully and said, "I follow your drift. You're saying that as word gets around about a peace officer with a serious rep and a nice ass, any hard cases riding in to test her mettle are likely to be harder than usual?"

Longarm couldn't resist answering, "I ain't seen the ass of either J. P. Keller or Undersheriff Reynolds. Have you?"

The Cheyenne lawman grinned dirty but confessed, "Wouldn't know either gal if I woke up in bed with 'em. But word around here is that few men would complain if they found themselves in such a surprising situation. Talk to two saddle tramps and you get three descriptions. But I've been given to understand both gals are grass widows. A gal would have to have a muley streak to carry on so mannish to begin with if you ask this child!"

Longarm hadn't. But it was a point worth considering. Divorced women were called grass widows because, single as they might be in the eyes of the law, they still had husbands above the grass instead of below it, like decent widows were supposed to.

There was nothing unlawful about a woman being a grass widow, as long as she didn't mind the gossip. They'd already told him Keller's Crossing was dominated by a few founding families, with pushy distaff members of the same taking more interest in local politics.

They both heard a hail and saw a distant hat being waved above the rim of that false front above the stationery store.

Casey said, "That's Pete's old cavalry hat. Pete rid with the cav agin Red Cloud back in sixty-six."

He called out that they wouldn't shoot. A bare head and some with hats peered over the top rim of that false front at them. So the two of them got up and headed across.

Casey muttered, "I just hate it when they shoot and run like fool roaches in the lamplight."

He called up, "Any sign up yonder, boys?"

Longarm was as surprised when the one called Pete yelled down to them, "Plenty. There's an old boy up here with half his face torn off. Looks as if he caught some pine siding and a key-holing bullet smack in the mouth. Not long ago, judging from all the blood still oozing out of him. But whenever or whatever happened to him, he's dead as you told us to take him, Marshal!"

Chapter 8

When Longarm and Marshal Casey joined the others atop the flat roof across the way, Longarm saw he'd guessed right about the Henry rifle the sneaky cuss had been pegging away with. It lay beside him on the tar paper as he stared up wide-eyed from his bloody mangled face. Longarm's return fire had left cat's whiskers of splintered sun-silvered wood sticking to the rasberry jam around his shattered teeth. But one of said teeth was gold, the staring eyes were oyster gray, and the heavy brows above them met in the middle.

The tan ten-gallon hat over by a smoke flue went with his fancy tooled Justin boots and buscadero gun belt. So Longarm wasn't too surprised when he hunkered down to find a tooled leather wallet on the corpse with a library card allowing he was Thomas Taylor out of Amarillo.

He told the other lawmen assembled, "This adds up to a serious want known bests as Texas Tom Hatfield. He had state and private bounties posted on him. We wanted him for robbing a post office. The states of Texas and Arkansas want him for back-shooting peace officers

57

in both jurisdictions. The Pinkertons are paying the most because of a train he robbed in Kansas.''

He rose back to his considerable height and turned to the town law to soberly add, ''I am telling you all this because I'm up this way with other fish to fry. My own boss frowns on his deputies filing for reward money. You'd be welcome to as much as you can collect on this son of a bitch if you wanted to claim him as your very own and save me some paperwork.''

Marshal Casey shot a sweeping look across the faces of his own men, there being no others up there with them, yet, and declared in a certain tone, ''The son of a bitch put up a hell of a fight when we asked him what in thunder he was doing up here with that infernal Henry and no hunting permit. But just for the private peace of my soul, Deputy Long, what in blue blazes was this all about?''

To which Longarm was forced to reply, ''I ain't sure. This rascal had a rep for back-shooting lawmen, on his own or for pay. Since I just recognized him as a wanted killer, he might have recognized me earlier and decided to kill me on his own. It's just as possible, and as likely, somebody else wanted me killed lest I be getting warm. If I knew whether I was getting warm or not I wouldn't have to guess so hard.''

He moved toward the fire steps they'd all climbed up as he continued, ''I got to get it on back to my hotel with a package I dropped across the way. Had this skunk known where I was staying, he wouldn't have been following me around. I reckon he, or they, were watching for me by the Western Union. That's where I'd watch for a lawman on a field mission if I'd just heard he was in town.''

One of the younger deputies started to ask how come the late Texas Tom had scaled those fire stairs with yonder rifle instead of just letting fly with it over by the telegraph office.

Before Longarm or Casey could reply, a more weather-beaten deputy snorted in disgust and said, ''He wanted to get away with it, you asshole. All sorts of folk point fingers at you when you gun a man on the streets of Cheyenne in broad-ass daylight. If he hadn't missed from up here, he'd have just laid low ahind yonder false front until his gunsmoke and the excitement faded away. Weren't you paying any attention when we shot it out with him, just now?''

The kid deputy grinned sheepishly and allowed he'd forgotten. So Longarm knew he was free to climb down from the roof and elbow his way against the current of the gathering crowd.

There was hardly anybody on the far side of the street in front of the notions shop. He saw nobody had lifted the brown paper package he'd thrown against the siding near the entrance. As he bent to pick it up, Daisy Gunn A. K. A Crawford joined him, breathless, barefoot, and back in her mannish duds, to sob, ''Oh, Custis! I knew you were mixed up in it as soon as I heard the shots and folk in the hall commenced yelling about a shootout betwixt lawmen and a rooftop sniper!''

Longarm grabbed her gently but firmly by one thin arm and frog-marched her inside, where the nice old lady was holding a broom as if to repel boarders as she wailed, ''Get out of here before I call the law, you ruffian!''

Longarm moved Daisy back from the front glass as he told the little old lady, ''I am the law and I only talked rough because you were in the line of fire, ma'am. This other lady, though you wouldn't know it, is the one I just bought them more ladysome duds for. Now, I have yet another business proposition for you. How much would you charge me to let my deputy, here, dress up more girlish and stay here with you as if she was hired help or a visitor from other parts?''

The older gal told him not to be ridiculous. Then, being a gal, she asked him what they were talking about.

Longarm explained, ''I am U.S. Deputy Marshal Custis Long. This here is Deputy Daisy Crawford. Like you can see, I've had her disguised as a boy because she's working undercover for the U.S. Government and me. Them shots just fired at me from across the way may mean the crooks we're after have been watching us a spell. Me and Miss Daisy were checked into the Pilgrim Hotel. By now the other side might know this.''

The older woman stared primly at the raggedy barefoot waif he'd just described as a girl checked into a hotel with him and sniffed, saying, ''You should both be ashamed of yourselves, working under cover or on top of the covers!''

It was Daisy who blazed, ''He ain't been fucking me, ma'am. He's been so pure it makes me want to puke!''

The older woman looked away, red-faced and trying not to bust out laughing. Longarm said, ''I ain't asking you to hide *me*, ma'am. I need a place to hide Deputy Daisy where I won't have to worry about her as I do some scouting ahead.''

She didn't look convinced.

Daisy asked what he was talking about, asking, ''Didn't you tell me we were fixing to sneak out of town together as soon as it got dark?''

Longarm nodded and said, ''I did, and like Mr. Robert Burns wrote, the best laid plans of mice and men get old and gray when the other side could be on to 'em. They may or may not know I checked into that hotel with a ragamuffin of indeterminate sex. Whether they've taken you for a sissy boy or a mighty rough gal, they'll be *expecting* us to still be together when, not if, they notice we ain't at the Pilgrim Hotel no more. So I'd be harder to spot, sneaking about alone, while you'd be harder to spot doing the same, in a whole new outfit, as soon as I figured it was safe to send for you, see?''

Daisy didn't. It was the more wordly shopkeeper who set aside her broom to explain, ''I see his plan and it makes a lot of sense, dear. He chose some much more feminine clothes for you, earlier. If we did something about those farm girl braids . . . Perhaps an upswept hairdo with just a little discreet powder and paint . . . I could introduce you as a niece I'm breaking in, unless you'd feel safer hiding out up in my quarters above the shop."

Daisy said, "Oh, Lord. I've been cooped up less than one day in a hotel room and it feels like being in a soft jail. I got this gun in my hip pocket if anybody comes in here after me."

Longarm and the older woman exchanged more grown-up glances. He shrugged and said, "I had to deputize her in a hurry. The right sort of help can be hard to find at short notice."

The little old lady smiled thinly and replied, "So I can see. May I consider myself one of your posse, or would you describe us as a harem?"

Longarm laughed easily and said, "My boss would never go along with that notion and, even if he would, I ain't a Turk nor Mormon, ma'am. So I reckon we'd best describe you as a concerned citizen, and how much is this going to cost the justice department?"

The little old lady said, "People who know me well enough to ask such questions call me Covina, Covina Rivers. If Daisy, here, is willing to help around the shop, make her own bed upstairs, and behave herself in general, we'll call it even. As you said, good help is hard to find."

Longarm said she had to charge Daisy's grub at the going army and civil-service rate of four bits a day. So they shook on it, and old Covina carried Daisy and her new duds to the back of the store, where she was supposed to change and stay put until quitting time.

As she drifted the other way with Longarm, she told him she knew how to make a tomboy look like a young lady. She suddenly blurted out that *she'd* been considered poised as well as pretty, one time.

Longarm smiled down at her in the doorway to reply, "You're still a handsome woman, Miss Covina. I've known ladies with older-looking faces who did wonders and ate cucumbers with a little help from a bottle of henna or sepia tincture."

She sniffed and said that would be a cheap trick. He

had no call to argue. Portia Parkhurst, attorney-at-law seemed sort of proud of her gray hairs, all over, as well. As they parted in the doorway he tried not to picture either sweet old thing allowing him even a peek at their pubic hairs by lamplight. He assured old Covina he'd wire complete instructions from wherever he might be when and if he thought it safe for Daisy to break cover.

As he made to leave, old Covina grabbed his sleeve and demanded, "Have you two been telling me the truth, about your relationship, I mean? She's really attractive, and a woman can tell when another woman is ready and willing."

Longarm sighed and said, "I'd be a liar if I said I wasn't willing, Miss Covina. I'm a natural man, and all men should be horsewhipped regular for the willing thoughts they have about you ladies. I ain't got time to explain why a lawman can't afford to indulge such thoughts with a lady who may have to back his play in a federal court. I told her why, and I'm sure the two of you will have plenty of time to jaw about each and every thing I've ever said or done to her."

The older woman showed how wordly she might be indeed by laughing lightly and declaring, "I guess that means there's no hope for poor little me, either, you unfeeling brute."

He laughed back and lit out, lighting up along the way as he told himself to stop picturing that nice little old lady buck naked. She'd likely been a looker as well as a prick teaser in her day. And he'd found what Ben Franklin had written about older women could come as a pleasant surprise, indeed.

Dr. Franklin, writing to a young diplomat in Paris, France, had advised him to take up with old French widow women instead of young wives who'd get them into duels or chambermaids who'd get them into trouble with their papas. Franklin had opined and Longarm had found it true that, just as a tree could turn funny colors from the top as the sap was still running sweet farther down, an older-looking gal could still have a lot of juicy life left in her while, above all, as old Ben had pointed out, they were more likely to feel grateful than sore at a man in the cold gray dawn.

Longarm laughed at himself and Ben Franklin as he strode on to the hotel with neither Daisy's duds nor Daisy waiting for him now. He had to go back, himself, to fetch his possibles, saddle, and Winchester. If he hadn't, he'd have holed up somewhere else, himself, until it was safer for certain to move on. For anybody who'd learned he was there in Cheyenne was as likely to know which hotel he'd checked into under his own fool name, leaving instructions for his home office to wire him there.

So he entered the Pilgrim the sneaky way and slipped up the back steps, where he discovered to his relief that the match stem he'd stuck in his door crack was still in place.

He let himself in, scooped up his load, and let himself out just as sudden after tossing both his and Daisy's keys atop the unmade bed for the chambermaid to carry down to the desk after check-out time.

He slipped down the back steps and out through the stable without a word to anybody. He carried his load the long way 'round to the livery across from the depot and bet a colored hostler they wouldn't store it for him until after dark.

Once he'd lost and seen his load safely stored in the tackroom, Longarm felt free to see what a man might be able to nibble, free, with an expensive scuttle of beer. He caught up with the town deputy they called Culhane at the free lunch counter in the Bullhead Saloon.

Culhane said they'd carried the remains of the late Texas Tom over to the Cheyenne morgue and taken all the credit for him.

Longarm agreed that had been the deal and asked in a desperately casual tone what a man who patrolled Central Avenue a lot might be about to tell him about Miss Covina Rivers at the notions shop.

Wrapping a slice of rye around a twist of jerked venison, Culhane replied without hesitation, "She owns the whole building. Started in Cheyenne after her man was killed in Red Cloud's war up north. He was an army suttler. They jumped him as he was hauling goods up the Bozeman Trail from Fort Laramie. I understand the army surgeon refused to let her view the remains after he'd tried to put them back together without much luck. But old Covina was left enough by her man's life insurance to start over on her own, and she's done well with the gals here in Cheyenne. My own woman shops there now and again. The prices seem right and the notions seem to be in fashion. I don't know why the gals change the way they dress every season. Do you?"

Longarm shrugged, said he'd been getting away with the same tweed suit since he'd bought it a good spell back, and decided he'd try the boiled eggs and pickled pigs feet.

Once he'd calmed the rumbles in his gut with free lunch and the surer knowledge he'd left little Daisy in fairly safe keeping, he still had time to wire Billy Vail about Texas Tom, unofficial but no doubt of interest to the old paper-pushing fuss.

Retracing his steps to the Western Union, Longarm picked up a pad of yellow blanks as he casually asked the clerk behind the counter if by any chance there'd been any reply to that wire he'd sent off to Denver earlier.

The clerk suprised him by nodding and telling him, "Your friend just picked it up for you, less than half an hour ago. Didn't he tell you?"

A big gray cat swished its tail in Longarm's stomach, and he was tasting pickle-brine as he quietly asked, "A friend of mine, you say? Might this old pal you handed my wire to have worn a ten-gallon hat and had a gold front tooth?"

The clerk shook his head and said, "Panama suit and a planter's hat. He was sweating just the same as he told me you'd sent him over from your place to fetch any messages. I naturally made him sign for it. I got his

64

name right here in this pad and . . . let me see, ain't he called Bordon Knox and ain't he riding for the same outfit with you?''

Longarm grimly replied, ''I'll ask him when I catch up with him. I reckon we just missed each other back at my hotel.''

Chapter 9

Longarm returned to the livery and got his Winchester '73 saddle gun before he headed for the vicinity of the nearby Pilgrim Hotel. It hardly seemed likely the sneak who'd signed for another man's telegram had used his own name. But Longarm did know a shady cuss called Knox—they called him Deacon Knox—from a friendly little game of cards in the Nebraska Sand Hills a spell back. That panama suit and planter's hat fit the way he'd have described the shifty tinhorn, too. But a Knox by any first name ought to stand out from tar roofing in white linen and bleached straw. So Longarm made his way along a back alley to another hotel across the way and catty-corner to the older Pilgrim. He broke out his federal badge and pinned it to the lapel of his denim jacket before he found a service entrance opening on the alley and strode on in.

Nobody seemed to care until he'd negotiated a dark hallway and mounted a flight of back stairs to the top floor. That was where he scared a full-blood chambermaid headed the other way with a feather duster. She asked what he was doing up there in spite of the badge pinned plain as day to the infernal front of him.

He hoped he had her nation right as he told her, "Hear me, I am *Akicita*. That is why I wear this *maza* on my chest. I have come because I am on a *hunblechia* and I have to get closer to *mahpiya!*"

The moon-faced but nicely built young Lakota gal said, "*Nunwey.* Let me show you how to get up on the roof. Why do you try to talk our way, when I understand your words and you say ours so funny?"

He said he'd been trying to be polite as she led him just down the hall to what looked like a broom closet and opened it to let him see more stairs as she explained, "We don't want guests going up on the roof, drunk or sober. Are you the lawman my people know as the *Washichu Wastey*? You look as I have always pictured him from hearing others who have known him."

Longarm modestly allowed some Lakota called him *Wasichu Wastey*, which would sort of translate as Good Trash, when you studied on it, because *Wasichu* was applied to white or colored folk with the same disdain by Lakota as some whites applied to folk of African ancestry. White reporters liked to translate *Wasichu* as "American" so that the great chief *Wasichu Tashunka* appeared in print as "American Horse" instead of "Stallion Stolen from Trash Enemies" as it fell on Indian ears.

He asked the Indian gal's rear what her name was as he followed it up the steep stairs with his Winchester. She said to call her Sue. He wasn't sure whether that was supposed to be a joke or not. Indians didn't laugh out loud as much as other breeds, but they could enjoy a pun as much as anyone.

Whether she'd meant Sue or Sioux, her trim figure was still outlined through her maid's black poplin skirting as she flung open the roof door to catch the afternoon sun from the west.

He told her to stay put. But she followed him out on the tar paper anyway, allowing it was a free country, her hotel, and she'd been set to quit for the day after making all those damned beds in any case.

Longarm didn't argue. He removed his distinctive Stetson in case anyone on another rooftop cared to take them for hotel staff, and when he didn't spot another damned soul on the lower roofs all around he asked her to hang on to his hat whilst he climbed the rungs of the water tower.

She took his hat, but said, "I think you are going to fall off and break your neck."

She didn't sound as if this bothered her.

Longarm had to allow she had a point as he mounted the weathered wrought iron rungs awkwardly, thanks to the rifle he had to carry up with him if his trip was to mean toad-squat.

By the time he'd reached the platform the big plank water tank was set upon, Longarm could see that despite the way it had puckered his asshole, his climb had not been in vain. For from up there he had a clear view of every other vantage point within rifle range of the front entrance of the Pilgrim Hotel across the way, and there wasn't a soul, in any sort of outfit, staked out as a roof-top sniper.

He gingerly made his way back down, it wasn't as easy, and took his hat back with a nod of thanks as he told the Lakota gal, "I know a bad man of my kind knows I'm still checked into the Pilgrim Hotel over yonder. If he wasn't sure before, he found out when he conned a telegraph clerk into giving him a wire addressed to me at my own hotel. So where would you be, right now, if you were laying for me to come back to my hired room at yonder Pilgrim?"

The *weya* calling herself Sue demurely replied, "I was not allowed to hunt with the boys when I lived on the reservation. That is one of the reasons I don't live on the damned reservation. Is it true you rode into one of our tipi circles, alone, after you had fought us and counted coup on young men you had killed?"

Longarm grimaced and said, "I had to. A renegade outlaw was hiding out with that band. I've never counted coup on any men I've had to kill, young, old, red, or

white. Gents who drive railroad locomotives get grease
and soot all over 'em. Gents who ride for the law have
to kill somebody now and again. You have to take the
good with the bad in any line of work. I wonder if that
mysterious stranger in a white panama suit could be
holed up in another hotel room, across from the entrance
to my own lobby.''

Sue said, "I don't know. I have not met many men
who could count coup but I don't want to. I used to get
so tired of listening to my father and brothers boasting
about all the wonders they'd performed before they
turned into fat reservation drunks with nothing better to
do but brag and brag and brag!''

Longarm didn't answer as he led the way back to the
stairwell. He knew what she meant. He'd been invited
to supper in a tipi more than once. Neither heroism nor
modesty were the same to most Indian nations as they
were to whites. Horse Indians such as the Lakota
counted coup for acts of what might seem cowardly cru-
elty to a white man, or took chances that struck whites
as downright *loco en la cabeza* because it seemed most
admirable to do something astonishing as all get-out than
to worry about the final results. So young men in search
of a rep were inclined to do the most outlandish things
they could come up with as they rode into battle, from
snatching a baby from its momma's arms and smashing
it against a tree to closing in on a full-grown armed
enemy and just slapping his face to ride off, laughing.

As the two of them made it down to the top hallway,
Sue told him she had a passkey to every room in the
place. He allowed rooms that overlooked the entrance to
the Pilgrim were most interesting to him at the moment.
So she suggested they start at the far end and work their
way closer to directly across from his own hotel.

He agreed and they did, skipping more than one because, she said, she knew the folk who were inside, snor-
ing or giggling, as the case might have been. Longarm
told her the boys back home should have let her go
hunting with them, adding, "I follow your drift about

anyone aiming to do me dirt having to hole up in an officially empty room. You'd have known right off if any cuss in a white linen suit and planter's hat was checked in here open and above-board, right?"

She unlocked one of the last chances, standing aside as Longarm covered the doorway with his Winchester, and said, "There is nobody like that staying here. But you got all the way upstairs without them seeing you down at the desk."

The room was empty as well as small. He still moved across it to peer out through the lace curtains. He grimaced and moved back to Sue, saying, "Clear shot. But mayhaps clearer from the next one, on the corner of the building, right?"

She shrugged and said, "It would be. But there is nobody there at this hour. The whore who rents that suite by the week is due back any minute. Her story is very funny. Every afternoon she goes up the street to make love to a banker in his office. The bank closes for the day at three. The banker goes home for supper at six after a hard day at his office. I know this because men count coup on things like that as well. The whore who spends her nights alone next door never told me. She is not a bad person, for a *wasichuweya*."

Longarm said, "I'll take your word for that. I'd still like to see whether there's anybody else in there right now. It ain't quite suppertime, and if you know she spends her late afternoons at the bank, a sneak brassy enough to declare I sent him to fetch a wire addressed to me might know it by way of the same sources, see?"

She did. She said she didn't like doing it. But it only took them a minute to sneak into the perfumed chambers next door and make sure the gal who'd stunk 'em up had no visitors or trespassers.

As Longarm turned back from the window, the young Indian gal was holding up a mighty realistic dildo carved from ivory, albeit hardly from life, unless there really was a natural man, somewhere in this world, with fourteen inches.

71

Sue waved the big ivory dick like a fan as she asked him what he thought it might be.

He smiled thinly and replied, "If you ain't never seen the real thing, it might be just as well to leave you in blissful ignorance."

She calmly replied, "Oh, I can see it's supposed to be some man's cock, and I've heard you *Wasichu* have big cocks, but do you really think even a whore with the *winyanshan* of an old *pte* could fuck a thing this big?"

He said, "Put it back where you found it. The gal who lives here likely counts coup with it for visitors. I mind this one old gal with burro, down Mexico way, but that's a whole nother story and I don't want to be caught by anybody in here."

They ducked outside and locked up. Longarm wistfully said, "So much for this hotel. I hope I can recruit me such a friendly guide with her own passkeys, next one over."

Sue said, "You can't. I can. They pay Indian help even less next door. So their upstairs maid dosen't speak enough English and you don't speak enough Lakota to get along this well with her. But I told you I was through, up here. Why don't we sneak down the back stairs and see what we can do next door?"

That was the best offer he'd had so far, and it went smooth as silk because it was just before quitting time, with the halls in all the neighborhood as empty as they tended to get.

Sue led him out to the alley and around to another back entrance. They went down to the celler, and Sue knocked on a door until a young but ugly Lakota gal peered out, sleepy or drunk, to mutter, "*Anigni ktey, wincincala! Hehetchey!*"

Sue was cussing back while Longarm was figuring out the sleepy-eyed gal had told them to go to hell because she was through for the day, albeit *anigni ktey* translated literally more like "Evil she-spirit take you, someplace awful."

Whatever she said back to the sullen thing, Sue soon had custody of another key ring by the time her cousin or whatever slammed the door in their faces and went back to bed or whoever.

Sue led Longarm and his Winchester up the back stairs only the hotel staff was supposed to use. That didn't mean he shouldn't keep a round in the chamber, of course. But they made it to the top floor without incident and, this time, started with a room almost directly across from the entrance to the Pilgrim.

Sue told him her pal in the celler had said none of the top floor rooms were in hire that evening. That left them a seven-door chore with a heart-stopping moment for each and every damned doorknob.

Longarm moved over to the window, which was half open because of the season, and glanced casually down at the street as it commenced to fill with quitting-time traffic. Then he gasped and moved back from the curtains as he spied a planter's hat coming out of the Pilgrim with a rumpled white panama suit under it.

As the Indian chambermaid joined him closer to the curtains and asked what was wrong, he pointed down at the outstanding figure in the crowd to declare, "That sure as shooting looks like a tinhorn called Deacon Knox that I know from Nebraska. But I'm missing some pieces, here. Deacon Knox was a card cheat and a con man, not any hired killer, the last time I looked and . . . thunderation, he's ducked around the damned corner, and I have to get down there before he gets away for good!"

It was the born food-gatherer who pointed out, "Hear me, rabbits run in circles, but fast. Too fast to chase, once they are out of sight. But if you wait they may circle back again, *ohan*?"

He started to object, nodded, and said, "When you're right you're right. All this time I've been pussyfooting around up here, he's been laying form down yonder, in my very own lobby!"

Sue said, "He has found out you are not upstairs. He

73

has started to wonder why you have not come home. Or maybe he has gotten hungry, himself. I think he is going to scout around the places one can have supper near the center of Cheyenne. The town is not too big for one man with good legs to scout. When he sees you nowhere else, he may come back to your hotel to see if you came back while he was looking for you. If you go looking for him on the streets of Cheyenne in the suppertime, the two of you might never meet before or after dark!''

To which Longarm could only reply, ''I have a damned night train to catch, too. I wonder if that's where he's headed right now. Seeing he's been so free about reading my messages.''

She pointed out, ''You have no way to cover both the railroad and that hotel. But hear me. When he does not see you getting aboard any train, he might come back here to see why. Let him be the rabbit who runs in circles, *Wasichu Wastey*. From up here you can see whether he comes back here after you or not.''

Longarm started to ask what happened if the mysterious tinhorn never came back at all. But he knew that was a dumb question. He'd be no worse off and it was likely safer to stay put up here where none of them could expect him to be, until such time as he could figure out where even one of them might be.

He told her as much. She moved to the hall door and bolted it on their side as she murmured, ''*Nunwey*. I am glad. Help me move this bed over there by the window.''

He naturally asked how come.

She said, ''Don't you want to keep one eye on that entrance across the street?''

When he allowed he did, she asked, ''Don't you want to have some fun with me while you're laying in wait for your enemy? In the Shining Times our young men often had to lay in wait for days at a time, and it was the custom of us *Lakotaweyan* to lay there with them and keep them from finding it too boring.''

Chapter 10

Longarm helped the enthusiastic upstairs maid shift the brass bedstead over to the window, as most men would have, but he felt obliged to warn her as they worked together that he might have to leave on short notice and couldn't promise he'd ever get back to her.

Sue said, "I know this. That is why I have not been waiting for you to blow your nose-flute outside my father's tipi or come by with a string of ponies. I don't want to marry any man before I have seen more of life as a woman running with the wind. I heard about that time you spent with some other Lakota women up in the land of the Great White Mother. I want to find out whether they spoke straight about *Wasichu Wastey* who never beats a woman and never leaves her feeling hungry, *hipi*!"

Longarm might have remembered *hipi* meant "here" if she *hadn't* let go the bedpost to grab at her old ring-dang-do and rub it good through her thin poplin skirting. For some reason that made him feel like rubbing at blue denim, but he refrained, being a man who could wait for his supper until he'd set down to the table, when it seemed they meant to serve it right!

The bedcovers came almost dead level with the windowsill, once they had the bedstead lined up with the same. Longarm didn't want to risk his Winchester rolling out the open window. So he put it crossways at the head of the bed, against the head rails, where it would be out of the way or handy, as the occasion warranted.

While he was doing that, she'd drawn the covers down and folded them neatly but swiftly less they wind-up spotted, as she delicately put it. There was something to be said for chambermaid experience when it came to making or unmaking beds.

There was something to be said for growing up Lakota when it came to doffing duds in broad-ass daylight, too. For Longarm was still fumbling with his shirt buttons after draping his gun belt over a bedpost when the tawny little gal dived across the mattress naked as a jay to roll face up with her chunky brown thighs apart as she asked him directly for some down-home *tawitan*. He knew that meant fuck.

He tended to learn the sassy words of any lingo first. Then she threw in some shocking gestures that made Longarm thankful for those lace curtains.

Summer sunlight lingered late at Wyoming's latitude, but he doubted anyone could see in through the wind-rippled cotton lace from across the way. So, not wanting them to hear her begging for it, down in the streets of Cheyenne, Longarm shucked his own duds to join her. It was easy, seeing she'd shoved a pillow under her firm brown rump to greet him with her legs flung wide as she could fling them.

He'd almost forgotten how swell that first thrust into a strange pussy felt, after all that purity around young Daisy and old Covina. So there was something to be said for staking out a hotel entrance Lakota style, as if he could have gotten out of it.

He knew what he was doing would have been a federal offense if she was still on the reservation, while turning down a Lakota gal who'd offered him some *tawitan* could takes years off a rude gent's life.

The awsome rep Border Mex gals enjoyed for being dangerous to cross was largely due to the Indian blood and folkways so many of them denied. Ladies raised by Latin traditions were prone to be murderously jealous but practical about how far a gal could carry on with her man. But Indian women, while far less possessive when they'd been brought up Indian style, were too stubborn to call it a day whenever you *did* push one over the edge into wailing like a banshee and throwing anything they could lift.

So it was just as well the spunky little Sue only seemed out to count coup with her pussy and satisfy some natural curiosity about a man her nation found confusing because he tended to treat Indians firm but fair next to some others, red or white.

Once he had it all the way in and commenced to rub himself all over her, inside and out, the hot-and-bothered fullblood cried out, "*Mitakuye oyasin!* They were right about you! You feel so good all over and there is so much of you to feel!"

Longarm tried to assure himself his boss down Denver way might agree this was in the line of duty, seeing they needed her help as much as she seemed to need a good reaming. So he kept on reaming and didn't stop when she stiffened, bucked, and said she'd just climaxed. He growled he hadn't, and when she protested her crotch was getting cramped from gaping so wide, he rolled her on her belly with one of the pillows under her hips to raise her brown rump admirably.

She felt even tighter inside with her legs down together between Longarm's own as he straddled them to enter her from a whole new angle. He'd have never managed, had not her rear entrance been so slick with renewed desire and past satisfaction. Once he had most of it in his own desire renewed considerable and the inch or so left out in that position as her smooth sweat buttocks clasped them from either side.

They both wanted to make it last, and that position offered Longarm a much better overlook at the hotel entrance across the way. He wondered what that sassy walking gal down yonder in the Dolly Varden skirts would say if she knew what was going on up here behind these nigh transparent curtains. He wondered why he was picturing her in this very position with her frilly skirts thrown up over her blond ringlets. But the chambermaid he was screwing felt the effects of such dirty daydreaming and allowed he was surely a natural wonder.

He knew he could keep going indefinite if he humped her at an easy lope and let his mind wander some from her own sweet twitchings.

So he jawed with her as he long-donged her, and she seemed flattered he was willing to discuss the mission he was on with her.

When he asked if it made sense to her that inexperienced shemales could track down experienced riders of the Owlhoot Trail, the Lakota gal arched her spine to swallow more of him as she calmly replied, "Hear me. The blue-sleeved eagle chief your people called Custer had been riding the war path long. Very long. They say he won many good fights in that war between the blue sleeves and the gray sleeves. They say he won all the battles he ever fought with those who paint themselves, until that one last battle where the greasy grass grows beside the wooded waters."

He stopped deep inside her, holding back as her soft wet innards throbbed around his turgid shaft, and asked her what in thunder the Battle of Little Big Horn had to do with inexperienced young gals. He asked, "Are you saying them ferocious fighters Crazy Horse led at full gallop along Last Stand Ridge were inexperienced shemales?"

She began to corkscrew her firm brown rump enticingly as she said, "They might as well have been, as far as the eagle chief you called Custer cared. They say his Absaroka scouts told him there were many tipis, many, where my own nation had met with others at a place with plenty of water and good grazing. They say the blue sleeves had some of those medicine guns that piss bullets in a steady stream. But the eagle chief left them behind, along with the long knives that might have saved some of his men when the fighting got hand-to-hand at the end. They say he divided his own war party into three columns before he knew how many of us he was dealing with. They say the fight atop that ridge where he made his last stand lasted less than half an hour as you people count such times. I think he must have been a very good war leader who knew what he was doing when he led his blue sleeves to their last fight.''

Longarm started to make an obvious objection to her odd line of reasoning. Then he followed her drift and started moving in time with her twisting as he declared, ''You're saying an experienced veteran of many an almost one-sided victory could get in a whole lot of trouble because he was so used to winning he never considered how he might lose! Custer rode to disaster that sunny summer day because it just never occured to him that enough Indians to overide a cavalry column could ever be gathered in one place and mounted up all at once. He knew all about fighting Confederate Cavalry and traditional bands of Horse Indians, no offense. Just like many a rider of the Owlhoot Trail may know, or thinks he knows, how to bust the law and evade the usual consequences. Jailbirds hardly talk about anything but what the two of us are doing, or how to put one over on the law. But they consider womankind when discussing pleasure and mankind when discussing how to get away with most anything else.''

She moaned she was coming. That made two of them, but Longarm was still able to mutter, ''I figured right off they were overconfident enough to let a girl-child get the drop on them. But how could even an overconfident crook leave a trail for the sweet little thing to follow without help?''

Then they were too busy to talk for a spell as Longarm rolled her on her back to finish right with her firm breasts plastered to his naked heaving chest and her open lips panting puppy-like in his face, Horse Indian style, while he came in her all the way down to his curled-under toes and quickly bent them the other way as his calves commenced to cramp.

As he lay soaking in her, with some of his weight politely on his elbows, Sue smiled up at him and said, "They had some man helping them."

He kissed her, his way, and asked if there was any point to what she'd just said. The Lakota gal replied, "To scout those outlaws so some *wasichuweya witko* could shoot them while they were wondering how to fuck her. Don't you see how easy that would be?"

He started to object, nodded, and kissed her some more before he said, "I think somebody may have just pulled something like that on yours truly. Somebody who knew me on sight, just as I'd know him, went pussyfooting around until he knew I was in town and could make some educated guesses as to where I'd pass through rifle sights. If some less than heroic bounty hunter or professional informant could track down a wanted desperado from a safe distance, then send for a pretty little thing to carry out the execution, a lot of pieces do fall into place. But to tell the truth, that theory leaves a whole new bunch of questions unanswered."

She switched her twat teasingly and asked what a theory was.

He said he was sorry he used big words when he was studying hard on a case and explained, "A theory is a line of educated guesses that might or might not add up to a proven fact. The jury is still out on Professor Darwin's theory about us evolving out of clams or something worse. The theory that there were Seven Golden Cities down New Mexico way has been proven false for certain."

She asked what the quests of Darwin or Coronado had to do with the case he was working on. Then she decided, "Never mind. I don't really want to know. I'm getting hot again. How do you feel about that?"

He said he had noticed a certain hardening in his attitude toward her. So they were going at it, slow and sensuous in the cooling draft from the open window beside them as they both knew without discussing it that they were really going to have to stop and rest a spell after this one.

It felt nice to just keep it hard enough to stay interesting in her as he reclined on one elbow, gazing out the window through the lace at the same time. The first stars were out and somebody had lit a streetlamp whilst they'd been too excited to pay attention.

That was something to study on. Even a familiar figure in a white hat and suit could slip in or out of a hotel entrance he was supposed to be watching in the time it would take to light a damned streetlamp.

He said so and she dreamily replied, "I don't care. I just want to keep doing this *hunkesni, owihankeshni!* Would it be better if I got on top?"

He sighed and said, "Nothing lasts forever and I dasn't let you get on top because I'm trying to keep one eye on that hotel entrance across the way."

She told him in that case to move faster, adding, "The *Wasichu* in *ska* may never come back. Or he may have already come back and you didn't see him."

Longarm growled, "I just said that. If he knows I'm still paid up at the Pilgrim he could be staked out, his ownself, anywhere on the premises! I ought to be whipped with snakes for carrying on this way whilst I'm supposed to be watching for Deacon Knox!"

Then he suddenly spotted a big blur of white moving along the far walk in the gathering dusk and paused in mid-stroke to declare, "If that ain't a paid-up member of the Ku Klux Klan after somebody else, it looks as if we guessed right about that son of a bitch scouting around town for this child in vain. Suppertime is clearly over, and he may figure I'm doing something like this, with somebody else, up in my vacated room across the way!"

She asked who else he had in mind. Then she wrapped her tawny legs around him and groaned, "I don't care.

81

Finish what you have started with me! Don't tease me! *Hi-yey! Hi-yey!* Faster! Faster!''

He knew it would be faster to finish than to try to take it out, even had he wanted to. So he pounded her hard to glory and enjoyed it so much he almost passed out beside her when she suddenly went dishrag limp and let her arms and legs fall free from him.

He rolled off her instead, feeling light-headed as hell when he sat up to start dressing. When she blearily asked what he was doing he didn't answer. She murmured, ''*Onsika*, you men are all the same. You would rather fight than fuck.''

Then she'd dozed off again and Longarm was on his feet in his old army boots, strapping on his .44-40 as he smiled down wistfully at the voluptuous tawny curves he might never see again and murmured, ''What can I say, Miss Sue? What can any man say at times such as these? When you're right you're right.''

She called him something dirty in Lakota as he gently but firmly slipped the Winchester from under the pillow her head was half dozing on. As he backed toward the door in the gloom, he could still make out the play of light through the fluttering curtains on her smooth warm skin.

As he eased out into the hall he muttered to himself, ''There really must be something wrong with me. For this ain't the first time I've passed on a whole night of fine screwing in favor of one son of a bitching get-together with another asshole with a gun!''

Chapter 11

Longarm circled wide in the gathering dusk to enter the Pilgrim Hotel by way of its connections to the stable out back. He snicked his Winchester off Safe as he eased up the back stairs to the dark upper hallway. They hadn't lit the hall fixtures yet. But there was enough light from outside to see the pale match stem on the darker hall runner near the bottom of his hired room.

He didn't try to open the door. He eased on by and used a certain blade of his pocketknife to open the cheap lock of the room next door he'd hired for little Daisy.

He followed the muzzle of his Winchester inside, crouching low, to see her room was empty. He moved through the gloom to the bath shared by both rooms. Daisy had naturally left the door on her own side unbolted because the bolts were on the insides of both doors for the sake of private bathing.

He glided across the tile floor on the balls of his feet to find that Daisy, bless her, hadn't bothered to bolt the door leading on into his hired room. She'd offered right out to fuck him, thinking back on such free-and-easy bathing.

The asshole-puckering part came next. There was no

better way to manage. So Longarm set the Winchester on the floor tiles and drew his six-gun for close-quarters chores as he gingerly reached for the bolt with his left hand.

He took three deep breaths, held the last, and hunkered down to charge into the room beyond in a crouch, crabbing to one side as he snarled, "Drop your hardware and grab some ceiling you son of a bitch!"

There came no answer. The room was empty. Longarm put his six-gun away with a sheepish grin, muttering, "Shit, just as I was starting to enjoy myself!"

He moved back the way he'd just come, picking up his Winchester and leaving by way of Daisy's door. He didn't bother to lock her door with his pocketknife. The hotel's keys were where he'd left them to be found by the chambermaid. He wondered idly what *that* one looked like as he moved down the front stairs, this time wondering why a man who'd just shot his wad in one chambermaid cared what yet another one might look like.

As any experienced housefighter knows, sneaking up a flight of stairs is way safer than sneaking down one. Because when anyone might be laying for you, up or down, your head popping suddenly into view offers a poorer target than almost all of you, pussyfooting down the stairs before your fool head can see where its going. So while the tall deputy and his Winchester tried to move quietly, they just went down the last flight of stairs in a sudden bunch, ready to return any fire aimed their way.

But as he got to the bottom, Longarm saw that nobody seemed at all interested in him. He could only make out some of the desk across the lobby and two ladies sitting at a dinky table under a potted paper palm between him and the front entrance.

So he circled the stairs he'd just come down to ease into darker shadows with his back against a solid wall. When nothing happened, he moved along the wall until, sure enough, on the far side of those descending stairs,

84

he spotted the white-clad Deacon Knox seated sideways to him in a big leather easy chair, smoking a cheap-flash cigar as if he didn't have a care in the world.

Longarm swept the shadows all around with suspicious eyes. But if it was a trap, it was a new one on him. He slid along the wall until he could beeline in to gently but firmly shove the muzzle of his saddle gun between the top of the chair and the back brim of that big white planter's hat.

Deacon Knox stiffened as Longarm warned in a conversational tone, "One twitch of your dick and your head winds up in a side pocket. For this ain't a pool cue I'm holding against your brains, you two-faced tinhorn rascal!"

Deacon Knox sighed and kept looking straight ahead as he replied, "Use your own brains, Longarm. Would I be sitting here like a big-ass bird with both hands empty on the arms of this old chair if I meant you harm?"

Longarm left his rifle muzzle where it was as he asked, "How come you picked my lock and tossed my room upstairs, you harmless cocksucker?"

Deacon Knox soberly replied, "I never went up there to commit crimes against nature or yourself. I've been waiting here a spell. Knowing you'd been marked for death, I finally let myself into your quarters to pay my respects to your remains, read your mail, or whatever. I saw by the keys you'd left on the bed you meant to be leaving town tonight. I've been all over town trying to catch up with you and tell you not to do that. I finally came back here because it occurred to me that since you'd asked your office to wire you in care of this hotel, you might come back to check with yonder desk before you left."

Longarm withdrew his Winchester from the nape of the tinhorn's neck and moved around to face him with the rifle pointed a mite less rudely. He reached for a nearby bentwood chair, spun it around so he could sit it astride while facing the older man in the easy chair,

Winchester across his spread thighs and .44-40 hanging handy, before he declared, "They told me about the con you pulled at Western Union. I'd like to read that wire you intercepted, now. Reach for it slow."

Deacon Knox smiled sheepishly and said, "I threw it away lest it be found on me. Your boss, Marshal Vail, wants you to meet with the county board of supervisors, convey his suspicions to the sheriff in command of the whole shebang, and head back to Denver unless you come across something really new. He says others have investigated other shootouts all over this great land without managing to indict even one of those Wyoming wildwomen."

Then he took a drag on his big cheap cigar and added, "What's a Wyoming wildwoman, old son?"

Longarm said, "I was hoping you'd be able to tell me. But let's talk about you. What the fuck have you been up to, Deacon?"

The tinhorn wistfully replied, "I wish I knew. I thought I knew until you bigger boys commenced to play too rough for this delicate child. You know me of old, Longarm. Did I throw down on you or try to get somebody else to gun you after you'd treated me so mean over Nebraska way?"

Longarm smiled thinly and replied, "I didn't treat you so mean. I exposed you as a cardsharp after I caught you dealing dirty to a lady. Nobody killed you. Nobody even arrested you. You and your pals were allowed to leave town in peace, as long as you left sudden."

Deacon Knox nodded soberly and said, "Then it's established we left peacefully. I told you at the time I didn't want to catch any north-bound trains because I'd met up with a rougher crowd up this way. But your pals gave me no choice and so that's what happened. I was sitting there minding my own business with a faro shoe in a back room when Texas Tom Taylor, who was really named Hatfield, caught up with me the night before last. Texas Tom and I went back to a summer on a Missouri road gang. We had little else in common. But he knew

I knew you on sight. So he offered to let me in on a good thing if I'd be willing to point you out when you came to town."

Longarm nodded and said, "I can see you pointed me out. What was the deal he offered for my demise, thirty pieces of silver?"

Deacon Knox blew smoke out both nostrils and gasped, "Be fair! I never played Judas on nobody! Lord knows you've never been no pal of mine! You damn near got me killed, myself, when you exposed the way I'd got so lucky at Slapjack in that dinky Nebraska trail town. But I was never out to get you or anybody else shot in the back. They told me they were out to *avoid* you, not to murder a federal lawman! I like to shit my pants when I heard how you'd shot it out with Texas Tom. I could have told him how safe it was to shoot at you, had he asked me. But he never! I swear to God!"

Longarm said, "Keep your voice down. Let's keep this private. You said *they* told you fibs about me. I only got Texas Tom. Who else am I gunning for?"

The tinhorn told him, "Ram Rogers and vice versa. Taller than you but twice as skinny. Dark hair, dark complexion, dresses dark, and some say he has some colored blood, but he says it's Cherokee. Soft spoken and slow moving, until he tenses up to slap leather. He's said to move like spit on a hot stove when he has to. I've never seen him kill anybody. I didn't even know he had that rep when I first fell in with the two of them, Dear Lord, just a few short days ago that seem like years!"

Longarm said, "Time flies when you're having fun and drags when you have a toothache. I know Ram Rogers by rep as well. His real first name is Melvin. That could account for the chip on his shoulder. I'd like more on that deal you mentioned, now."

Deacon Knox said, "You've heard of the Big Rock Candy Mountains beyond the Seven Cities of Cibola, and naked hula-hula dancers of the Sandwich Islands who just can't do enough for white gods off whaling ships? Well, there's this one crossroads cow town up along the North Platte run by a ladies' sewing circle with even the town law in skirts!"

Longarm didn't grin back as he said, "Keller's Crossing. What about it?"

The tinhorn scowled and said, "I just told you. There's hardly any menfolk guarding the two banks in town, the stagecoach terminal, the railroad freight and passenger office and Lord knows what all. The town's on an all-season ford across the changeable North Platte, where a railroad spurhead connects with stagecoach traffic coming down from the Montana gold fields along the old Bozeman Trail, now that the army's reopened the same after putting Mister Lo, the poor Indian, in his proper place."

"I know about rich passengers and gold dust changing to the railroad at Keller's Crossing." Longarm cut in, adding, "Are you saying they offered to cut you in on armed robbery in exchange for my ass?"

Deacon Knox shook his head and answered, "You know I do my robbing with a deck of cards. Texas Tom told me the gang him and Ram Rogers were riding with planned to take the whole township over, lock, stock and barrel, see?"

Longarm said, "I don't. Other menfolk would never allow it. They may or may not share your views on the qualifications of the weaker sex to hold public office. But I just can't see a gang of big tough boys busting in on a sewing bee to simply take the premises over. A good loud scream from just one of the upset shemales would surely bring other boys running. The county, if not troops from Fort Laramie, would be moving in on your pals before the dust settled."

Deacon Knox said, "Nobody said nothing about taking the township over the way the Cheyenne took and held Julesburg a few hours, that time. The bunch Texas Tom and Ram Rogers told me about mean to take over just the *running* of the township for keeps. They've seen it's an inbred clique of four or five widow women who've managed to squat on all the lily pads in a modest pool. Most of the men just working in and about Keller's Crossing have been too busy to worry about who's running the town, as long as it's been running smooth. I was told the plan was to buy out or scare off a few helpless widow women and replace them with men who share the views of the gang and the late Sheriff Henry Plummer, up Montana way.''

Longarm whistled softly as that pragmatic approach to wealth sank in. For the notorious Sheriff Henry Plummer and his deputized stage robbers had almost gotten away with it!

The wild career of Henry Plummer had begun around Nevada City, California, when he'd gunned the man of a woman he admired, back in the early days of the California gold rush. He beat that charge but got arrested soon after for killing another man while he was robbing a stagecoach. But he busted out before they could hang him, and the next anyone heard of him he was a vaguely sinister young man with no visible means of support around Lewiston, Idaho. Before his past could catch up with him, he'd moved on to the new Montana gold fields and run for sheriff during the confusion of the war back East.

Longarm fished out a smoke of his own as he told the tinhorn he was starting to worry about his wild tale. He said, ''If Henry Plummer could get elected sheriff while more responsible men were too busy to bother with local politics, anybody could do it. Plummer was wanted on every charge but farting in church. But they elected him, and in less time than it takes to tell, he'd gathered close to two hundred outlaws from all over to rob the stages he earmarked with chalk after asking the management, in his capacity as sheriff, which ones were most worth robbing.''

Longarm lit his cheroot and added, ''Had he been content just to get rich, he might have gotten away with it. But once you rob so much that business comes to a standstill, folk commence to study their neighbors harder. Once the vigilantes whupped a full confession out of one member of the Montana Innocents, as the gang was called, old Plummer and ten or twelve other ringleaders were invited to the same evening rope dance. But they'd sure lived high before they'd hung high, and some would-be mastermind is always trying to repeat the past performances of some earlier mastermind who might have gotten away with it—if only.''

Longarm took a thoughtful drag on his smoke, let it out, and demanded, ''Where do I find said mastermind so's I can ask him?''

Deacon Knox shook his head and said, ''You shot my main contact with the outfit. Texas Tom knew me well enough to tell me where we'd be meeting next. I suspect Ram Rogers and the gal he has holding his horse, or his dick, depending, must have been spooked as me when you nailed Texas Tom with a head-shot, blind, at that range!''

Longarm shrugged modestly and said, ''It just takes practice. Let's talk about why Texas Tom was up on that roof to begin with. Have you any notion why my arrival in Cheyenne made them so morose?''

Deacon Knox shook his head and said, ''I told you they never told me they meant to kill you. The deal was for me to point you out so's they could steer clear of you.''

''Didn't anybody say why they wanted to steer clear of me?'' Longarm insisted.

The tinhorn thought back, then tried, ''Ram Rogers said something about you being there when Rusty Mansfield was gunned, down Denver way. He said you'd had the chance to talk to any number of witnesses, and there was just no telling what you'd heard or how warm you might be.''

Longarm grimaced and said, ''I'm flattered as hell. But I purely wish I had the least notion what he suspected I might know. Because all I know for certain is that I'm *missing* something about all this!''

Chapter 12

Longarm had long since learned not to warn a suspect of a possible slip by following up on it too tight. Every time he'd pressed Deacon Knox about his own intended assassination, the tinhorn had insisted neither the late Texas Tom nor the still armed and dangerous Ram Rogers had taken them into their full confidence. So in the end he'd told the slippery Deacon they were square and advised him to get out of Wyoming Territory while he was ahead.

After he'd done that he'd circled back to tail the white-suited sneak in the tricky flickersome night-lights of downtown Cheyenne. But while it was easy enough to keep an eye on that linen suit and big white hat from a discreet ways back in the early evening street life, Deacon Knox spoiled it all by having a couple of stiff drinks at a saloon near the depot and then going on to the same to pay his way out of town aboard the next westbound U.P. as if he'd been paying attention to Longarm's fatherly advice.

Longarm doubted it would be prudent to pussyfoot any closer to the railyards, recalling what Deacon Knox had let slip about others guessing he was bound for Keller's Crossing and knowing which night train was most likely to get him there. The tinhorn was likely on the level about not wanting to be mixed up in the killing of any man who rode for Billy Vail and the attorney general of the whole U.S. of A. But it would have been expecting too much of a born crook to ask for the finger-pointing rascal to point a finger at his erstwhile chain-gang mate. Old Deacon had doubtless described Ram Rogers the same as the wanted fliers posted on the surly breed because he'd known the lawman he was talking to had surely read at least one.

But since he only knew Ram Rogers by description and ill repute, and had even less on the shemale accomplice who could be staked out most anywhere, Longarm had to reconsider his immediate travel plans.

A stranger in town didn't lay low in waiting rooms, saloons, or an all-night chili parlor. As he drifted back from the part of town those rascals would expect to see him in, he considered returning to that hotel across from the Pilgrim to see whether little Sue still liked him. But parting was a sweet pain in the ass when you only had to do it once and he wasn't sure he could get it up again with a block and tackle if Sue *had* stopped cussing him.

He'd missed his supper during all the earlier excitement, and now that he found himself and his Winchester hugging the shadows with nothing better to do, he felt hungry as a bitch wolf hunting prairie dogs.

But all the places he passed that served grub were lit up inside like display cases for the perusal of any gunslick shopping for a target along the darker walks. So there had to be a better way.

It came to him as he'd circled aimlessly, or so it had seemed, to the stretch of Central Avenue where he'd had that shootout with the late Texas Tom.

He'd already decided not to hole up with any other lawmen there in Cheyenne before he was certain where those gunslicks Deacon Knox had been with knew anyone else with an ear to the neighborhood gossip. He'd never told anyone he'd been told to stop over in Cheyenne for some courtesy calls on other lawmen. Whatever the gang's leaders had heard about him being in the Parthenon Saloon in Denver at the time of Rusty Mansfield's death by gunfire, they *should* have expected him to arrive that afternoon on the passenger varnish and lay over by the depot just long enough to catch the earlier local he'd been forced to miss. Not the night freight that only went as far as Fort Laramie.

As he stood on the plank walk in front of Covina Rivers's notions shop, dark and shuttered at this hour, it came to him she and little Daisy were no more than a door knock away. So he moved to the side door betwixt the shuttered front window and that now half-empty rain barrel to knock on it.

A familiar voice from inside called out, "We're closed for the night. You'll have to come back in the morning!"

Longarm called back that he didn't want to buy any ribbon bows or yard goods, and his voice must have seemed familiar, too. Because old Covina opened up to greet him at the bottom of the stairs in a flannel robe with a candlestick in one hand and her long gray hair down.

She said, "Daisy and me have been pulling taffy in our nighties. What on earth brings you here at this hour? You told us you'd be out of town aboard that late local."

Longarm replied, "I noticed. Since last we discussed my travel plans, I've changed them some, and even worse, it seems somebody out to gun me knows my next move by the time I can manage to make it."

She told him to come inside before somebody saw her talking to a man in her nightgown with her hair down, land's sakes.

As he stepped inside, he could smell hot buttered taffy, and he'd never known he liked the sticky sweet shit that much as his empty stomach rumbled.

She led him up the narrow stairs as he told her what he'd been up to since that afternoon, leaving out his friendly meeting with the Lakota nation but telling her what Deacon Knox had said about hired killers hiring others to finger him there in Cheyenne.

She gasped. "Heavens, you say you even suspect your fellow lawmen, Custis?"

To which he replied, "Not all of 'em. Maybe none of 'em told any drinking pals that much about me with any malice aforethought. You know how idle gossip makes its rounds until somebody with way more interest overhears it. I know neither you nor Daisy could have told Deacon Knox and his pals I was planning on missing that last afternoon local up to Keller's Crossing because I thought I'd make it, as I was leaving here, earlier. I had time to catch my intended train when I found out someone had been acting cute and could be laying for me at the Pilgrim Hotel. Their tinhorn scout gave up when I hadn't shown up by the time I should have left town. When he rejoined his pals, they told him they'd been watching at the depot and I still had to be in town. So they figured I meant to catch the later train tonight and sent him back to the Pilgrim to see what else he could find out."

By then they were up in her kitchen, where young Daisy sat grinning in her own nightgown, from the stock below, fooling with a cabbage-sized wad of sweet sticky goo.

Covina told her to put it back on the stove for now and turned back to Longarm to ask, "You say this member of the gang *told* you all this, Custis?"

Longarm removed his Stetson and hung it on a kitchen hook as he replied, "Not hardly. He switched sides sudden when I got the drop on him and likely scared him honest. He swore he hadn't known they had orders to gun me. He'd now have it known he was simply a poor dishonest cardsharp who fell in with the wrong companions. His conversion may be sincere. Old Deacon Knox has no rep as a gunfighter, and it must have been a sobering experience to have me nail his pal Texas Tom and get the drop on him with this Winchester, all within hours. I chose to believe his sad story because I didn't want more paperwork on my plate, and it was just as easy to run him out of town. I knew Deacon Knox ran out of town easy, and I suspect he'll keep running.''

Daisy asked if he'd ever been to bed with two women at the same time.

As old Covina blushed beet red, Longarm refrained from bragging to reply, ''Right now I'd rather have something to eat, no offense. I've had no sleep and barely enough grub to go with the hard day I've put in since leaving Denver a million years ago, and Lord knows when I'll ever get there at the rate I've been going!''

Covina turned to her kitchen range, allowing there were still some coals left from their taffy making, as Daisy asked why Longarm didn't spend the night with them and get an early start in the morning.

Covina hushed her but volunteered, ''I do have extra rooms and so wouldn't it be a good idea to lay over here until those killers lose interest in that railroad depot?''

As she broke out a skillet and a smoked ham he could already taste, Longarm shook his head and said, ''They ain't being paid to lose interest, and I'd lose yet more time in vain. My boss wants me up in Keller's Crossing. Their boss don't. They've had plenty of time to stake out the railyards, and they're likely staked out comfortable for as long a wait as they want.''

As she sliced ham for her skillet and got out a basket of eggs, he continued, ''I only know one of them by description and rep. He has at least one shemale with him who might be better at recognizing me in tricky light than vice versa. In sum, they have the deck stacked to their advantage, and even if I won I'd be tied up here with the paperwork too long to catch that way-freight. It'll be pulling out before ten and then where would I be?''

The gray but fine-figured Covina put the ham on to sizzle first as she calmly replied, ''Safe here with us? Why do you keep calling that last train out to the north a way-freight? I know what a freight train is, but I'm not sure I've ever heard one called a way-freight.''

It was Hobo Daisy who chimed in from her own perch across the table. ''Silly, a way-freight is a local that makes every stop along the way. They run them when the passenger varnish and fast freights ain't using the track, which is usually single line betwixt towns, out this way.''

Longarm chuckled and told Covina, ''That's about the size of it. Night-crawling way-freights ain't much. But they purely beat walking, or even riding, once you're talking about any distance. The old iron horse keeps chugging long after a regular horse is through for the day.''

As a heavenly smell of frying ham filled Covina's already sweet-smelling kitchen, Longarm mused, half aloud, ''Already thought about hiring myself a bronc at the livery across from the depot for some serious riding. But it's too far to push a pony, or even a rider, at any speed.''

Covina busted eggs over his ham as she countered, ''If I understand way-freighting correctly, there's an alternate north-bound leaving later and stopping at Crow Bend, eight or ten miles up the line, and closer by beeline across the range.''

Longarm nodded but said, ''Already considered that, Miss Covina. But they likely have the livery staked out, along with my fool saddle in its tack room. I'd have never stored it close to the depot if I'd gotten Deacon Knox to talk earlier. I could likely beg, buy, or borrow another saddle as well as a mount to shove under it if I had more time. But, like you said, we're talking eight or ten miles, and I'd barely beat the iron horse with a real horse if I started right now!''

Covina tipped his ham and eggs on to a china plate and served him as she told Daisy to pour the coffee while she tended to something in her bedroom.

As she left, Daisy stood close enough for Longarm to smell the fresh-scrubbed flesh under that chenille nightgown as she filled a mug for him, murmuring, "I think she likes you, too. Wouldn't it be fun if the three of us all got naked and had us a party?"

He laughed and told her to behave herself, having no call to tell her about the party he'd just had with a more-than-enough frisky Lakota.

The ham and eggs were swell. The strong coffee offered to see him through the next few hours of the night. But then what? He could ask for help from the local law or Billy Vail's sullen opposite number. But that would only make the outlaws crawfish back into their hidey-holes and tip their leaders off that he was on his way past them, even if he made the damned way-freight without having to jaw half the night away.

So mayhaps it was just as well, he thought, that he wasn't hard up enough at the moment to be tempted by a night in bed with two women. For Daisy's sassy suggestion made as much sense as trying to sneak past any number of owlhoot riders without knowing who they were or where they'd be laying for him!

He was sponging up the last egg yolk with a chunk of rye bread when Covina Rivers came back in, fully dressed in a tight-waisted navy velveteen riding habit, a bitty boater perched atop her pinned-up steel-gray hair, to ask if he was finished yet.

Longarm rose from the table to allow he sure was and ask if she meant to ride somewheres at that hour.

Covina said, "I keep my shay in the carriage house of a livery a block up the avenue. I don't drive enough to keep my own carriage horse, but I know all their good ones by name. So let's be on our way. If the one they call Blue Ribbons hasn't been driven this afternoon, she ought to get us there in plenty of time!"

Longarm was in no position to argue. He picked up his Winchester, grabbed for his hat, and followed her down the stairs as, behind him, Daisy wailed she wanted to go, too.

As he legged it up Central Avenue with the surprising

fast-paced widow woman, Longarm asked why she hadn't told him sooner.

She said, "You men are all alike. I'd have never gotten you to eat a warm meal and put away that much coffee if you'd had any hope of beating that way-freight to Crow Bend."

He had to allow she was right. Long before they'd gotten the long-limbed chestnut, Blue Ribbons, hitched up to her private two-wheel shay, he was telling her they weren't going to make it. He was sure of this as they trotted out the north-west city limits in the moonlight, along the service road that followed the single tracks and sandy Crow Creek toward the Laramie range to the west. For as spunky as she trotted, Blue Ribbons wasn't going to average more than nine miles an hour, and even a way-freight rumbled across the prairie at better than twelve between towns.

Covina explained the tracks followed the easy route of the creek as it meandered across rolling prairie. He didn't ask why when she reined Blue Ribbons off the service road and out across open range in the moonlight. She drove with skill many a man might have envied, and Longarm would have told her, had not they been bouncing so hard on the seat of her one-horse shay as they tore across the prairie in the tricky moonlight.

He didn't have to urge her to whip Blue Ribbons with the rein ends as they both heard a locomotive whistle in the distance, albeit not as far a distance as Longarm would have asked if he'd had anything to say about the matter!

Chapter 13

They made it with less than five minutes to spare. As the gallant Blue Ribbons panted head-down between the shafts, Longarm helped the hard-driving widow woman down from her shay and kissed her without thinking before he said, "I want you to promise me both you real pals will head back to Cheyenne at a walk! I got to run down the platform and talk to the freight agent now. I'll wire more detailed when I send for Daisy."

Covina flustered, "When and why? She's not a bad girl, but she's had no upbringing and seems terribly stupid, even for a sort of white Topsy off a farm."

Longarm said, "You work with what you have to work with, and I just said I'd wire more detailed instructions, once I know what I want her to do or say on arrival. I don't know what I'll find waiting for *me*, up the line, myself. So thanks a heap for the buggy ride, and I got to move it out, ma'am."

She asked, "Would you kiss me again? Just to say goodbye? I was caught off guard by that first one, Custis."

Kissing any gal never took as much time as telling her you didn't want to. So he took the nice little old lady in his arms and gave her a good one, sort of surprised but not upset when she kissed back French.

Old Ben Franklin had warned younger jaspers things like that might happen around nice little old ladies, Longarm reflected as he legged it along the platform to where some dim figures were gathered near the only lantern at their end.

When he showed his badge and introduced himself to the small-town freight agent, he was told the line would be proud to ride him up to the North Platte as long as he didn't get in the way. So when the way-freight hissed in to a short stop a few minutes later, Longarm set his Winchester aside and helped them unload a mail-order piano before he swung aboard the caboose with a wave back down the tracks to any lady who might still be there. You couldn't tell with the moonlight and inky shadows shifting so in the night breezes.

He'd been asked to stay out of the way. So he found a seat on the rear platform and lit up as they followed the tracks away to the north from Crow Creek, hugging a contour line of the now not so distant Laramies, a sort of orphan range running in line with but apart from the main thrust of the Rockies.

They passed a ranch house with the lamplight from the windows somehow making a passing stranger feel left out. Longarm had assured himself often enough that he wasn't really missing anything when he lay snugabed with a train whistle calling far off in the night. But it often seemed to promise new thrills and adventure in some far-off parts he'd never been while, contrariwise, whenever he was *riding* a train through the night, he got to wondering what he might be missing behind those cozy lamplit window curtains he was passing with no chance to ever ask.

He laughed and told the Winchester in his lap, ''The man of that house back yonder is likely stiff in the joints from working all day, and even if he does feel like turning in early with the lady of the house, she'll likely tell him she has a headache.''

He found himself wondering how long it would take good old Covina to get home, and what she and little Daisy would talk about when they got back to pulling taffy or went to bed in those flannel nightgowns.

He laughed at himself and told his Winchester, ''I reckon I've about recovered from that Indian campaign if I'm starting to picture nice little old ladies in flannel nightgowns or, better yet, nothing at all, and wouldn't that be a party!''

He'd seen enough of young Daisy to picture her buck naked in bed with him and French-kissing Covina. The way-older widow had as narrow a waist but fuller breastworks and bottom than the mature but not that mature Portia Parkhurst, attorney-at-law.

He snorted in disbelief at his own wild imagination and allowed he might as well imagine an orgy with all three of them, seeing it would never be more than a fantasy.

So he did and it was giving him one hell of a hard-on when the way-freight stopped again at Horse Creek to unload a ton of barbed wire and some crates of preserving jars.

And so it went as the night dragged on, with Longarm really feeling the hours since last he'd slept solid by the time they got as far as Chugwater, winding like a damned old snake and stopping at tiny towns with names humble or grand.

The brakeman came out on the platform to smoke with him as they rolled out of Wheatland. Longarm asked how soon they'd get in to Fort Laramie. The brakeman told him he was on the wrong line.

Longarm said something dreadful about railroad lines in general.

The brakeman soothered, ''You told us you wanted to go to Keller's Crossing, a day's ride up the North Platte from Fort Laramie. So it's just as time-consuming either way. We don't run a train this late along the spur that leaves Cheyenne to the northeast to hit the North Platte at Torrington and cut west to follow the river upstream. So you're saving hours this way, even though you have to catch a coach going downstream, from Wendover, if you want to wind up in Keller's Crossing. Think of the rails as the main lines of a spiderweb with stage lines the cross webs, at this stage of the game. Some day they'll likely have tracks and telegraph lines strung all over from town to town, but right now a man has to sort of zig and zag his way across this world.''

Longarm sighed and said, ''I've been zigging and zagging until I'm too tired to keep my damned eyes open. But I reckon the time I might have saved this way will make up for the last few dusty miles. And wouldn't most Wyoming hands expect me to grab that other feeder line out of Cheyenne to Keller's Crossing?''

The brakeman took an expansive drag on his own smoke and confided, ''The gent who said there was more than one way to skin a cat must have rid the rails out our way, some. Folk new to the territory are always confounding old *Fort* Laramie with the newer *township* of Laramie, eighty miles to the southwest, albeit still on the same North Platte river because of the way it hairpins around the Laramie Range. Eastern greenhorns and even old cowhands are always getting off at the wrong Laramie stop. There's two Virginia Cities you can get to by rail, and you want to get off this train at Wendover, Wyoming, not the one on the Utah-Nevada line way off to the west.''

Longarm asked if the stage line the brakemen had advised him to catch at Wendover was the same one running down the Bozeman Trail from the northern gold fields.

The brakeman said it surely was and cautiously added, ''Might you not be the same federal deputy who bummed a ride north from Denver early this morning with One Thumb Thurber on the Burlington Line?''

Longarm nodded but marveled, ''Lord have mercy, was it really less than twenty-four hours ago? Maybe I ain't making such slow time, after all.''

The brakemen said, ''I heard some Burlington hands

talking about your dust-up with the Black Swede, Gus Bergman. One Thumb thought he had it coming when you threw him off that rattler. He'd told the Swede not to mess with you.''

Longarm shrugged and said, "So did I. I suspect there's a screw loose inside his thick skull.''

The brakeman chuckled and said, "So did the Cheyenne dispatcher for the Burlington Line. He fired the Black Swede when he limped into town, demanding the railroad swear out a theft-of-service charge on a federal officer invited to ride free.''

Longarm said, "I suppose I ought to feel more pleased to hear the man lost his job. He surely wasn't meant to handle it. But I can't help wondering where a congenital bully with a temper he can't rein in ought to look for work to occupy his restless nature.''

The brakeman said, "The Black Swede seems to think he has to kill you before he worries about anything else. That's the real reason I came out here. If you say I told you I'll deny it. But the boys say you're all right, and Gus Bergman ain't your average hot-tempered bully. He's killed more than one man, and they weren't all unarmed 'bos. Gus packs a double-action Harrington Richardson .38, concealed.''

Longarm said, "I know. He showed it to me. But I thank you for your timely warning just the same. If you knew right off who I had to be, the Black Swede might have figured I'd be hopping a night train out of Cheyenne, and unlike some other rascals after me, old Gus may be far better at figuring railroad time tables. You say the natural place for me to drop off this platform would be Wendover on the North Platte?''

The brakeman allowed it was, if he meant to make connections with a stage coach to Keller's Crossing.

Longarm took a last drag, snuffed out the smoked-down cheroot, and decided, "I have to hire both a mount to get around and a saddle to replace one I wasn't able to get at, this evening. Once me and this Winchester are mounted up, it won't really cut much ice whether we ride into Keller's Crossing from any expected direction or not. What's the stop before we reach the river, and how far from the North Platte may that leave me?''

The brakeman said they'd stop at the trail town of Dwyer, seven or eight miles this side of the spurhead at Wendover. He thought and then volunteered, ''You might wind up *saving* a few miles if you ride east from Dwyer on a hired mount, now that I study on it. For we'll roll on to hit the river at a thirty degree angle at Wendover, so—''

Longarm cut him off by fishing out two fresh smokes and offering one as he said, ''I'll get off at Dwyer, and I'm much obliged, pard.''

The brakeman declined the offer and got back to his feet, saying he had to go forward and get back to work. So Longarm knew he owed the older gent more than idle gossip about the Black Swede. His railroad pals had spread the word that he might be in deep shit.

He put the two smokes away, unlit. Smoking too much when you were tired or hungry only seemed to make you feel worse, and his ass was really dragging now.

He didn't feel any fresher when the way-freight stopped at the dinky foothill settlement of Dwyer late as hell. He forced himself to wake up and help the crew unload some crates and a windmill kit before he asked the freight dispatcher there if there was a hotel to be had anywhere in town.

Everybody but the friendly older man he asked laughed like hell. The freight agent said, ''I reckon we could put you up for the night, Deputy Long. There ain't no hotel this side of Wendover, and the one there is notorious for its bedbugs.''

So that was the way Longarm found a place to catch up on some overdue shut-eye, snug in a featherbed on clean sheets under a thick old comforter that really came in handy before morning at that altitude.

Only men with nothing important to do slept long after cock's crow. So, seeing the freight agent and his mothersome old woman had acted so insulted when he'd offered to pay for his bed and breakfast, he went out back and split a day's worth of stove wood before breakfast.

The lady of the house still felt free to fuss at him and make him wash behind his ears at the pump out back while she made flapjacks for him, her man, and their four well-behaved kids.

Longarm was sorry to say goodbye to such folk, who'd more than lived up to the lamplight through their window curtains. But he had to, still tasting the buckwheat, butter, and sorghum syrup he'd washed down with strong black coffee.

There wasn't any Western Union in a town that size. He might have been able to patch through to their lines by way of the railroad's own telegraph net. But the more he thought about it, the less he realized he had to report, and he was getting tired of having others read his infernal messages. They'd said in a copy of *Scientific American* he'd read that someday private homes might be hooked up to a web of Bell Telephone wires more tangled than those of Mr. Cornel's Western Union. But until that day when nobody would ever be able to intercept private messages, a man had to study on what he put out on the wire for many a sneak to filch, the way Deacon Knox and Lord only knew who else might have.

He strode over to the horse trader the freight agent had advised him to try, Dwyer being too small to support a town livery, and found the trader and two of his rougher-dressed hands out in the paddock, gentling a young cowpony with a blindfold and feed sack.

The trader, called Bronco Bob for some reason, went on gently rubbing the proddy pony's spine with the man-scented feed sack while his boys steadied it and Longarm explained his predicament.

Bronco Bob looked dubious until he suddenly brightened and asked, "Might you be the same Custis Long as scouted for the Cav and the Wyoming Militia over in the South Pass Country during Buffalo Horn's reservation jump a summer or so back?''

When Longarm allowed he'd been there, but hadn't killed Buffalo Horn, personal, Bronco Bob laughed and said, "By Jimmies, you must be the only white man riding with us who *don't* count coup on that old renegade. I've killed him more than once when in my cups. You say you need a horse and saddle? You're going to need a saddle boot for that Winchester as well, and I've got just the ticket, if you ain't too proud to fork an old Cavalry McClellen.''

Longarm soberly allowed he wasn't out to rope no cows. So Bronco Bob told one of his hands to quit fooling with that damned halter and go saddle up old Socks, who turned out to be a buckskin standing a good fifteen hands on her four pale hooves. She looked as frisky as her owner bragged.

When Longarm asked how much all this was going to cost him, the horse trader bristled and demanded, "Do I look like a durned livery stable swamper? We rid against Buffalo Horn together, and you say you need the borrow of a horse and saddle. There *is* a livery over yonder at Keller's Crossing, next to the stage terminal. Leave Socks and my old army saddle there when you're done with 'em. I get over yonder regular, and I never charged Uncle Sam any bounty on Buffalo Horn, now that I study on it.''

They shook on it and Longarm had to fight the urge to say something mushy about a little trail town called Dwyer, which would never be famous as Deadwood or Dodge because the folk who lived there were so much more neighborly.

Chapter 14

The rolling sea of grass trended down some from Dwyer and the Laramie Range behind it. So the buckskin made good time under him as Longarm rode her east-northeast toward the flats of the wide but shallow North Platte.

Travelers' tales allowed the North Platte was a mile wide and an inch deep. This was stretching it some, at low water in high summer during a drought year. But it was true you could wade, ford, or drive stock across most any stretch that wasn't quick-sandy a good deal of the time. A good deal wasn't often enough for folk who crossed the North Platte regular. So Keller's Crossing had been surveyed, staked, and claimed where the river purled wider and shallower over a natural submerged causeway of bedrock.

Longarm knew he was getting warm long before he could make out a whitewashed church spire and barn-red grain elevator because he and old Socks took to passing clumps of grazing cows, mostly Texas Calico with a few black Cherokee Longhorns, and then he had to dismount to unstaple a drift fence because they'd been beelining across pathless open range, and the fence had been strung to keep uninvited stock west of it.

He stomped the slack wire flat in the tawny summer-cured buffalo grass, led Socks through, and tethered her to a post on the far side while he restapled the wire with a gun butt so's they could go on.

All the barbed wire they encountered east of the drift fence had been strung around quarter-section hog and produce spreads settled to supply the transportation hub ahead. So Longarm never had to ride more than a furlong either way to swing around a corner post. From time to time they'd catch a wave in passing a soddy, pen, and windmill complex. But Longarm would just wave back and ride on, knowing there was no way to rein in closer for directions or gossip without staying long enough for two helpings of coffee and cake. He was in a hurry and still tasting that sorghum syrup whenever he burped.

He walked Socks up the rises and trotted her down, trail-breaking at a cottonwood-lined prairie creek to put some water in her and get rid of some of his breakfast coffee. Then they rode on, topped only a few more rises, and saw Keller's Crossing laid out in all its glory on either side of the broad braided river down yonder.

His low-flying-bird's-eye view cleared up the hazier picture he'd had in his mind's eye. The simply laid single line of the other railroad that would have taken him longer ran along the south bank of the river on ties laid flat on the flood plain with little or no ballast. It was likely under water and surely under deep snow a good part of the winter months. But nobody shipped beef or produce in the winter, so what the hell.

The town, mostly private homes and two-story business blocks of frame construction, sprawled north and south of the river crossing with that grain elevator, a lower water tower and a couple of acres of stock-pens at the south end of the north-south main street and river ford. That tall white steeple and a few more imposing homes with mansart roofs rose from the north half of town, where stage coaches from the Montana gold fields reined in on that side of the crossing.

Having been through many such a trail town, Longarm would have bet money the quality folk and highertoned businesses would be found on the far side, upwind of the stock pens and railroad spur.

But there was only one way to be certain. So Longarm rode on in, with his loaded and locked Winchester riding crossways across his thighs and his last trail-smoke snuffed, lest even a wiff of smoke get in his eyes as he swept all sides ahead of him with an expression of calm he didn't feel, knowing somebody in that infernal town ahead had posted hired killers in Cheyenne to keep him from getting this far. And knowing his unknown enemy was sure to feel might chagrined from the moment anybody in Keller's Crossing announced his arrival!

Someone always announced the wonder of a stranger riding in on his own betwixt rail or stage arrivals. Longarm had given up the notion of riding in as somebody else as soon as he'd considered it. For his secret enemies would be on the prod for any stranger fitting his description, while the usual small-town pests would be more apt to start up with an apparent drifter than a paid-up lawman. So he'd pinned his badge to his denim jacket in plain view to avoid any words that might be awkward to take back. He suspected he'd made a smart move when he rode past the first neighborhood grocery near the south end of town, where a motley group of shabby men and one fat woman in a cheap flashy dress had clustered on the front steps to spit and whittle. He got dirty looks from some of the men and a sassy gesture from the flirty fat gal. But nobody yelled anything calling for a dismount.

He rode on past trashy frame houses and some boarded-over and shut-down shops and saloons. Business picked up between the open railroad platform and the shallow ford. But he saw nothing in the way of a public office. So when he came upon some kids throwing 'dobes in the river ahead, he reined in to ask for directions.

The kids knew more about digging 'dobes with their

penknives than the running of their township. Like kids in Denver, Omaha, and other parts of the stoneless high plains, they'd been raised busting windows and dusting heads with clods of dried mud, or adobe, available in such endless supply that high-plains kids had 'dobe fights about as often as they had snowball fights, albeit it smarted worse to get hit with a missile only a tad less dangerous than a solid rock.

Longarm hit pay dirt when he thought to ask them where their jail was. Small-town kids always pointed out jails and whorehouses to new arrivals.

They told him the jail was just beyond the stage terminal across the river. So that was where he rode, finding the North Platte barely fetlock deep this long after the last good rain, and reined in where, sure enough, they'd erected a small brick jailhouse next to a bigger frame building declaring it was the local substation of the county sheriff's department. So he reined in, dismounted, and tethered old Socks to the rail out front before he and his Winchester strode on in.

A teenage deputy dressed as if for Buffalo Bill's road show sat at the center desk in a fringed buckskin shirt, despite the season. He had buck teeth and a weak chin for such a mop of straw-colored hair and whispy mustache. But he didn't sound as stupid as he looked when he allowed they'd been expecting Longarm and added that his boss, Undersheriff Rita Mae Reynolds, would recieve him at her town house over by the churchyard.

As he wrote the street number in his notebook, Longarm asked how come they called the lady's house in town a town house, as distinct from any other house in town.

Her kid deputy explained that undersheriffing was only a sideline with Miss Rita Mae, who ran eighteeen hundred head of beef a hard ride off to the northeast, on old Sioux Treaty land.

Longarm agreed it made sense to have quarters at both ends of a hard ride. Then he casually asked if their

110

mighty active undersheriff had been running cows or running for office first.

The kid said Miss Rita Mae had been in college, back East, learning about business administration and such, when her uncle Clay Reynolds had up and died childless, leaving her the herd he'd just driven up the Goodnight Trail to the greener grass of Wyoming Territory. The kid said Miss Rita had been asked to accept her appointment as the township's undersheriff by the Cattleman's Protective Association. She being a member, even if she wasn't a man.

Longarm smiled thinly as he listened in to a smoke-filled room in his own head. He'd warned some other ladies they might not be thinking too far ahead with all this clamoring for rights and responsibilities. It was doubtless a bother to be told from birth that gals weren't allowed to play some games. But speaking as a man who'd dodged many an army shit detail and been stuck with the death watch at more than one public hanging, Longarm knew how anxious men in position to "Designate Authority" could be to pass the buck to anybody they could volunteer for a tedious chore.

The Wyoming Cattleman's Protective Association met in the new Cheyenne Social Club and prided itself on being modernistic to the point of that newfangled Arts and Crafts furnishings and the first electric lights west of the Big Muddy. So they'd naturally be slick enough to put one of their own in as sheriff and appoint dimwits or smart but willing gals to lesser positions of responsibility. It was the wave of the future, to hear all those women's suffering gals go on about how awful it was to let men have all the dangerous jobs.

As he went back out front, Longarm saw they had a hotel across the way, doubtless meant for travelers laying over between stage and rail connections, or buyers coming out here to the end of the rails in search of cheaper beef to ship. He saw they had a taproom with one street entrance, and it had been an all-morning dusty ride from Dwyer and that other rail line. But Billy Vail hadn't sent him all this way to drink on duty. So he forked himself and his rifle back across old Socks and rode on.

He shoved the Winchester in the saddle boot provided by his Dwyer pals as he saw how noonday strollers along the main street stared at him. Once you knew the range would be less than thirty yards in either direction, a six-gun fired faster and handier, anyway.

He saw the storefronts to either side looked more prosperous than the ones south of the tracks. Most were frame or even brick, this close to said railroad. For neither the sod walls you saw north of the Arkansas nor the 'dobe one you saw on the high plains south of same stood up to the ferocious weather out this way as well as balloon frame and shiplap sheathing. There didn't seem to be as many saloons as your average trail town would support. But that was their misfortune and none of his own, seeing barbershop gossip was more reliable as a rule.

He spied the imposing address on the far side of a half-empty churchyard and rode along its picket fence, absently reading off family names because he'd found folk with kin under imposing tombstones tended to run things a day's ride out in all directions.

The kid deputy had allowed they'd been expecting him. But Longarm was surprised when a colored boy in serving livery came out front to take charge of his mount as he was still dismounting.

The boy asked Longarm's permit to take Socks around to the back and stall her with fodder and water. Longarm said that was jake with him as long as they made sure the thirsty mare had her fill of water before they fed her anything dry.

The boy had been taught his place. So he never told Longarm such needless instructions were insulting to an old pro of fourteen.

Another servant opened the front door as Longarm mounted the steps of the imposing front porch, framed between two sort of castle towers sheathed in shiplap

112

and painted sunflower yellow with cream trim.

Longarm was led to a side parlor, where a vision in sky-blue silk with auburn hair piled high and only a little suntan to show for her riding back and forth rose from the spinet she'd been practicing on to greet him with a smile and wave him to a silk upholstered sofa he hesitated to sit down on in denim jeans.

As the servant, a sort of motherly colored mammy instead of the butler she could doubltess afford, headed back to the kitchen to fetch them some refreshments, the glamorous Undersheriff Rita Mae Reynolds, for that was who she really was, asked Longarm why they were still holding her deputy, the murderous little Ida Weaver, in connection with the shooting of Rusty Mansfield in Denver.

They both sat down, with Longarm's hat in his lap, as he told her nobody was holding any Keller's Crossing gals in Denver. He said, "Our law clerk carried her to the Union Station personal and saw her off on the afternoon northbound, day before yesterday, Miss Rita. She should have arrived long before this child, having almost a full day's start."

The swell-looking undersheriff of perhaps twenty-six or -seven summers stared at him with thoughtful amber eyes he felt like drowning in, as if she thought he was hiding something, while she insisted the other pretty girl who'd gunned that outlaw had never come back.

Longarm frowned thoughtfully and truthfully replied, "I wish I'd known that before I left Cheyenne last night. With one thing and then another I wound up all over Cheyenne, talking to all sorts of folk, but I didn't know I was supposed to ask if anybody had seen little Ida Weaver. So I never."

The motherly colored servant came in with a silver salver of tea and shortcake with the serving-trimmings as Longarm was asking the lady of the house what she knew about the late Texas Tom or his pal, Ram Rogers.

Rita Mae thought about it before she shook her glorious head to reply, "I don't have any wants or warrants on either name. Should I?"

She commenced to pour as Longarm said, "They tried to stop me in Cheyenne. As you see, they didn't. They were working with a cardsharp called Deacon Knox. How about him?"

The mighty refined peace officer replied, "We don't allow cardsharps in this township. One lump or two, Deputy Long?"

To which Longarm replied, "I'd as soon take tea straight, and my friends call me Custis, Miss Rita Mae. I saw some shut-down establishments down by the tracks and stock pens. But how you police your own jurisdiction is no never mind of my department. I reckon you know they sent me up your way to investigate this outbreak of desperados being shot down like dogs, all over this country, by Wyoming wildwomen packing warrants and badges from these parts?"

The beautiful undersheriff smiled alluringly at him as she handed him his cup and a wedge of shortbread, saying, "Of course I do. I'm rather proud of coming up with such an easy way to rid the West of so many disgusting old things."

So there it was, as plain and simple as a puddle of dog piss on the rug with her smiling as innocent as a pup who'd never been house broke, and now the question before the house was what they expected him to *do* about it.

He said, "You'd best start at the beginning, Miss Rita Mae. A heap of other peace officers have been alarmed by your draconion notions on law enforcement. But I try to keep an open mind until I've heard the whole story."

She nibbled as much shortcake as a mouse might have, washed it down with her own tea, and began, "*My* friends just call me Rita, and it all began last March with a shooting in one of the rowdy saloons I hadn't managed to shut down yet. The victim was a young Irish railroad worker. His killer was a brazen bully who'd just been paid off for a cattle drive and got to drinking and bragging as he waited for his train ride back to the Texas Panhandle.''

Longarm thought, nodded, and said, ''That would be the late Amarillo Cordwain, shot down like a dog by a sweet little thing as he was on his way to another man's funeral in the rain, right?''

The beautiful but mighty unusual peace officer nodded innocently and confessed right out, ''I didn't know what I was going to do about our own killing before that Irishman's weeping widow came to me with her aching heart set upon vengeance. As I'm sure you've noticed, I'm not a gunslinger. I hold a postgraduate degree in business administration. I run my substation here in town the way I run the beef operation left to me by a dear old wild and woolly cattleman. I've hired a good crew of experienced cowboys to manage my home spread and herd. They don't give me enough to hire the sort of lawmen I'd choose, myself, for my deputies. I don't have a man over twenty backing my play, as others might put it. None of the nice young boys I have to work with have ever been in a gunfight with a real killer. They can patrol the town and surrounding range for mad dogs and petty thieves. There was no way I could send anyone on my regular payroll all the way to Texas with a murder warrant to serve on a really mad dog like Amarillo Cordwain!''

Longarm said, ''We can talk about a murder warrant issued by a local J.P. later, Miss Rita. Tell me how you tracked that first killer all the way to Texas without any experienced manhunters at your beck and call.''

She answered, simply, ''That part was easy. The nasty Texas rider made no attempt to cover his tracks. Everyone knew he hailed from the Texas Panhandle, and he was down there bragging on killing a fool Harp up Wyoming way.''

''Who's everybody?'' Longarm insisted, adding, ''I understand how a friend of a friend of a man who works in a barbershop might spread such gossip, but sooner or later you ought to be able to backtrack it to the one who got the ball rolling.''

She thought and decided, ''I was told by Mr. Tanner, the owner of our own *Riverside News*. You'd have to ask him who told him. We've gotten such tips from newspaper men, railroading men, and just men riding through. As you just said, a friend of a friend tells a friend, and a man wanted dead or alive shouldn't be walking about bold as brass just because he feels he's safe across a few state lines!''

Longarm sipped tea thoughtfully and decided, ''I've heard a heap of gossip about Senator Silver Dollar Tabor, his imposing Miss Augusta, and that mighty sassy Baby Doe married up with another gent entire. I ain't sure just who told me what, now that you've reminded me. So it's easy to see how you could find out where an owlhoot rider had wound up without recalling just who'd told whom. Tell me how come that Irish mourner wound up shooting her man's killer down in Texas, ma'am.''

Rita said, ''I told her she could. She wept and swore and tore her bodice when I explained how little I could do about a killer so vile and so far away. When she hissed like a serpent that she'd be after shooting the gobbeen herself if she was a man and all and all, it suddenly came to me that there was nothing on the Wyoming statutes preventing a distaff undersheriff from swearing in another woman as a deputy. So I did and you know the rest. Armed with a warrant and a pepperbox .36, Deputy Maureen found it childishly simple to take the train down to Texas, ask about for the handsome devil, Amarillo Cordwain, and simply shove her pepperbox in his smiling face and pull the trigger one time!''

Longarm said, ''Once as he was standing and five times more as he lay oozing brains at her feet. I told you I read the reports, ma'am. Who told her to serve that warrant on him so direct?''

Rita shrugged and said, ''The feeling was mutual. The

distraught Maureen O'Boyle gave me the idea when she said she'd shoot Cordwain on sight. I was the one who suggested she hide her feelings until she could work her way as a helpless female within point-blank range.''

Longarm whistled softly and said, ''They sure taught you how to delegate at that business school. My boss, Marshal Vail, has already said admiring things about your delegated authority getting the drop on unsuspecting hard cases. Let's talk about the others, now.''

She seemed willing, not holding anything back as she went on and on about nine such executions in all.

As Longarm and others had surmised, the combination of a remote location and all that cross-country traffic passing though a tighter than usual bottleneck had conspired to attract the attention of more than one dangerous tinhorn or out-and-out road agent. When Longarm told her what Deacon Knox had said about some mastermind inviting crooks from all over the West to a township with a lady undersheriff, Rita sighed and said she and her own pals had suspected as much.

Then she said, ''Things have actually started to ease up, after the rash of robberies we had earlier in these parts. I'd like to think my sending girls to do what many consider a man's job had something to do with it. We were out to prove it was just as dangerous to break the law around here as anywhere else. I thought we were winning. That stage holdup pulled by Rusty Mansfield and some others was the last highway robbery in this county, and that was over a month ago.''

He asked about the latest Texas killer killed down Texas way since the killing he'd witnessed in Denver.

She explained, ''That was an argument over cards. Pecos McBride was another trail drover cut from the same rough cloth as Amarillo Cordwain. I don't know what gets into Texas riders when they're a long way from home. At any rate Pecos McBride shot a young homesteader in the taproom of the Pronghorn Hotel, right across from my substation. He rode out of town at full gallop, after dark, before my helpers and I could posse up, as you bigger boys put it. But, as in the case of Cordwain, the brute had told others here in town where he hailed from. It was Waco, nowhere near the Pecos, by the way. I recruited a girl I met at the homesteader's funeral to run down there and kill him back, the mean thing. She and the boy McBride killed over a penny-ante pot were engaged to be married.''

She saw the deep thoughts in Longarm's gunmuzzle eyes and asked him what he found so complicated about what she'd just told him.

He said, ''I'm studying on things you told me earlier, Miss Rita. It all sounds so simple until I ask how come your Ida Weaver never came back after I saw her gun Rusty Mansfield in the Parthenon Saloon the other day. The tale she told us jibes with what you've been telling me. But if it's all so simple, how come she's vanished into thin air, and why have other owlhoot riders been trying to prevent this mighty unrewarding meeting we're having this very afternoon?''

She said she wasn't sure she hadn't just been insulted.

Longarm said, ''There's nothing wrong with you, your shortcake, or this tea, Miss Rita. But you ain't told me a thing your Deputy Ida couldn't have told us down Denver way if my boss hadn't let her go without pressing her because he's so smart. He thought I might be able to catch you ladies at something more sneaky. He ordered me to mosey up this way, talk to all you Wyoming folk, and tell him what I thought you might be up to.''

She looked confused as she replied, ''But you just said you found this conversation pointless.''

He shook his head and explained, ''Not *pointless*, ma'am. Everything everyone I've talked to tells me points in the same direction. A tad rough-hewn and you'd all be in trouble if you'd been treating regular small-town pests so rough. But they told me in Cheyenne you'd all been warned not to word them arrest warrants so drastic and—''

''I've never written out any arrest warrants!'' she cut

in, adding, "I told Judge Edith it would look more seemly if she simply wrote she wanted us to bring the accused in for questioning. My temporary manhunters didn't need written instructions not to take any chances with a dangerous male gunfighter, for heaven's sake!"

Longarm shrugged and said, "Whatever. What I meant to say was that I'd have gotten here yesterday, we'd have had this conversation, and I'd have been headed home as bemused as them other federal deputies from the Cheyenne District Court, if somebody *other* than yourself wasn't trying to convince me he, she, or it was eating cucumbers and performing other wonders."

She said she had no idea what he was talking about.

He said, "The notion of a criminal genius is an affront to common sense. You have to be stupid or warped to want to ride the old Owlhoot Trail to begin with when you're all that energetic and clever. But the crooks chewing the fat in a prison cell or house of ill repute are forever convincing themselves they're masterminds and pestering us until we pay attention to them."

He washed down the rest of the shortcake he'd been handed and went on to say, "Hardly anyone had ever heard tell of Frank and Jesse James while they were robbing close to home and hiding out amid the trash whites of Clay County, Missouri. They had to clever themselves into a raid on Northfield, Minnesota, and wind up shot to pieces with their names in all the newspapers coast to coast. Billy the Kid, down Lincoln County way, could have drifted off an unremembered saddle tramp had he been willing to quit when Governor Lew Wallace put his foot down and declared the Lincoln County War was over or else. Crooks are forever getting distinguished tattoos, wearing odd outfits, or just bragging a heap about how big and bad they are until somebody like me gets the chore of tracking down such shy violets. You've explained how you and your deputy gals were able to track down some of the wildmen who tore through here. Deacon Knox explained how some self-styled mastermind has spread the word there's easy picking up this way, thanks to you being a gal and all, no offense. So how come they didn't just quit, if they were worried about somebody like me riding in to back your play?''

She poured more tea for the both of them as she decided, ''I think they think you might know more than you really do. You were there when our missing Ida shot Rusty Mansfield. You and those other Denver lawmen interviewed her right after the shooting. You had the outlaw's cadaver and personal belongings handy to go over as often as you liked. I know you don't know why they must have intercepted Ida before she could get back here to tell us something. But they must have had *some* reason, and they must fear you and me could figure it out if ever we compared notes like this, see?''

Longarm smiled wearily and replied, ''I wish I did. I've gone over that shooting in the Parthenon a hundred times in my head. I've jawed with other lawmen about all your Wyoming wildwomen, no offense, and to tell the truth I'd have given you the same bill of health as the boys from the Cheyenne District Court if those rascals you say you never heard of had only left me alone!''

He sipped enough of that extra cup to be polite and asked directions to where Edith Penn Keller, J.P., might be holding court that afternoon.

The lady undersherrif explained they didn't rate a courthouse in Keller's Crossing. The lady J.P. who rode herd on local legal proceedings from marriage licenses to arrest warrants took care of such matters in the front parlor of her own house off the main street but handier to the river crossing, stage terminal, jail, and such.

Longarm allowed he could likely find the place and started to rise, hat in hand. Then all hell busted loose.

''Down!'' he shouted as a bullet shattered the panes of the bay window across from their sofa to thunk into the papered wall above a head of auburn curls!

He let go his hat to draw his .44-40 with one hand and grab Rita by one shoulder to haul her out from behind her coffee table and down to the Persian carpet with him as another round spanged another pane of glass and hit the wall close to where *his* head had just been!

He hissed, ''They're trying to draw us over to that window! We need another one, higher up, and already open if you can think of one!''

She could. Longarm followed her shapely sky-blue rump as she led the way on hands and knees while yet another bullet whizzed over them from outside, just ahead of the echoing gunshot. It sounded like a rifle, over a hundred yards away. He didn't tell Rita. He was sure she had enough on her mind.

Out in the hall, where it was safe to rise, Rita waved back her motherly housekeeper and a bewildered-looking colored man in kitchen whites, yelling, ''Get everybody down in the celler! We seem to be under attack!''

As she headed for the stairs, Longarm called to the other grown man, ''I'm the senior law, here, and forget what she just said. Before you herd the rest of the help clean out of this wooden firetrap, I want you to make sure that front door behind me is bolted fast on the inside, hear?''

As the male cook moved forward to carry out his order, Longarm ran up the stairs after the lady of the house. She led him into a third-story sewing room up in one of those round towers he'd admired on the way in. She didn't have to point to the window opened wide to catch the prevailing summer breezes from the northwest. He told her to stay back as he eased closer with his six-gun, wishing like hell it was the rifle he'd left with that fool saddle!

But once he was peering around the edge of what he sure hoped to be a good solid frame, there didn't seem to be anything worth shooting at. He had a clear field of fire out across the churchyard as far as the looming whitewashed church itself. But if anyone had been up in the belfry with that rifle they'd be long gone by now. For half the town seemed to be coming from all directions with their own guns drawn as they shouted back and forth.

He told the pale-faced undersheriff it looked as if the mysterious rascal had just shot and run.

She murmured, "I hope so. I see what you mean, now, about them refusing to just let you be! But didn't you just tell me, down in the parlor, you'd about lost interest up this way?"

To which he could only reply, "That was then. This is now, and I am really starting to get sore!"

Chapter 15

Longarm tore down the stairs and out the front door with Rita Mae Reynolds paying no mind to his telling her to stay put in her house. That was the trouble with allowing Women's Suffering.

They found a reedy old cuss in clerical garb arguing with a heavyset gent in a summer weight Madras plaid suit on the front steps of the church across the way. The preacher was yelling at the huskier-looking cuss to do something, right now, about the front-door latch.

Rita introduced them to Longarm as Preacher Shearer from the manse on the far side of the church and Big Jim Tanner, owner and editor of their *Riverside News*. The minister was bitching and moaning about the way someone had jimmied the front door of his church, closed during working hours on a weekday. It wasn't clear what Preacher Shearer expected a newspaper man to do about this, and Big Jim said so, in the tone one usually reserves for small children and army mules.

Longarm had no call to explain his methods to the older cleric. He elbowed his way between them to just open the damned door and go on in, his .44-40 showing the way with its muzzle.

There was nobody lurking amid the dark varnished pews. He was sort of tense, and he yelled at the auburn-headed undersheriff more than once as she poked around after him with her own .40-caliber Patterson Conversion. He had as much luck getting her to stay downstairs when he worked his way up into the bell tower, ready to throw down on the first damned pigeon who cooed at them.

But all that remained on the top landing was a thick crust of dry pigeon shit, with the kitchen-match smell of gunsmoke lingering to explain why all the birds had flown away. Three spent brass .45-70 shells shone fresh-from-the-box on the shitty floorboards.

"Likely an army issue Springfield. About as easy to trace as a Stetson hat or a pair of Justin boots."

Rita peered past him out the open latticework pigeons could whip in and out through. She said, "I can see what's left of my poor bay window from here. But how could the villain have seen either one of us, inside, from up here?"

Longarm said, "He, she, or it couldn't. The plan was to draw me to yonder bay window where I'd have been in their sights at less than three hundred yards. Anybody watching from up here would have seen me coming to call on you. Anybody with any notion of the way your house is laid out would know that bay window goes with your front parlor. It don't take a college degree to read the little sign the shooter left us, Miss Rita."

She demanded, "How could anybody follow you up the street in broad daylight with a rifle, then break into the front door facing in the street downstairs without being seen?"

Longarm said, "I doubt it was done that way. When they failed to stop me in Cheyenne, they figured I'd get through and they knew I'd have to pay a courtesy call on yourself. So at least one of them got in downstairs before sunrise and waited up here, mayhaps with a good book, a jug of wine and somebody singing beside him, until I came along as expected and all went as planned until I failed to rise to the bait in your bay window."

She frowned thoughtfully and objected, "The shooter had to *leave* by broad day, didn't he?"

Longarm nodded and replied offhand, "We'd best scout around down below for his or her cheap rifle. Anyone willing to leave one behind only had to step out a side door into the churchyard and join the rest of the rush toward your shot-up bay window."

She gasped. "Then it had to be somebody who wouldn't stand out as a stranger in our township!"

Longarm managed not to sound sarcastic as he replied, "I somehow doubted we were searching for three wise men on camels, ma'am. Deacon Knox told me some local mastermind has been sending for outside help with a view to robbing you all blind. He, she, or it has to be somebody who's been here long enough to know Keller's Crossing and vice versa."

She forgot her ladylike manners enough to mutter, "Shit! That means there's little point in asking Western Union to tell us who wired whom from Cheyenne about you, doubtless in some criminal cypher!"

Longarm said, "It's worth a try. My boss likes me to use what he calls a process of eliminating. I doubt anyone would be dumb enough to use a cypher because that would be easy to spot, next to code."

She said she thought a code and a cypher were the same.

He pocketed up the spent brass and explained the difference while he helped her down the steep steps, saying, "You ain't the only one, Miss Rita. What most everybody calls the Morse Code ain't no code at all. It's cypher, which is a series of individual signs or symbols standing for letters of the alphabet. Don't matter whether you use dots and dashes, numbers or substitute letters. Anyone else can see at a glance the message is encyphered, and that's why crooks hardly ever use cyphers. Anyone as smart can figure your cypher out in time, once he knows he ought to."

She didn't seem to be following his drift.

He said, "A coded message is tougher to crack because it ain't half as easy to see it's in code. Codes are most often substitute *words* or sentences agreed upon in advance or written down in code books used by the sender and receiver. If somebody in Cheyenne wanted to tell a pal here in Keller's Crossing somebody like me was coming or not coming, they only have to word innocent-sounding messages a tad different. A message allowing Aunt Rhodie's goose had died in the millpond or from getting hit on the head with a walnut would only seem important to the ones who knew a millpond meant yes and a walnut meant no.''

Rita brightened and said, ''With Aunt Rhodie's goose meaning you, to them and them alone, right?''

He shrugged and said, ''If that was the code they'd agreed on. What will you bet they're using *other* code words and phrases?''

As he helped down the last step inside the tower, she dimpled up at him to declare, ''We can eliminate the majority of folk in these parts who haven't been sending or receiving telegrams at all, right?''

He shook his head and replied, ''Wrong. It's a sure bet that most of the folk in these parts have to be innocent. But a real sneak could send a coded message by wiring somebody innocent to *do* something, with a confederate watching for them to do it. I told you codes could be tougher than cyphers to break.''

As they stepped out into the church nave, one of her kid deputies came over to them holding a beat-up old trapdoor Springfield with as pleased an expression as a tabby cat delivering a dead sparrow to its mistress.

He said, ''We just found this in the flower bed by the side steps down to the churchyard, Miss Rita. That door bolts from the inside, and guess how we found the barrel latch? Looks like the jasper as shot out your front window got in here by forcing the front latch, then left by that side exit to slither and sneak his way through the tree-shaded tombstones to parts unknown!''

The newspaperman, Big Jim Tanner, joined them to ask who they were looking for in connection with this latest outrage. Before Longarm was able to nudge her, the lady undersheriff said, "Deputy Long, here, is of the opinion we're after a hired gun called Ram Rogers and at least one companion. They were in cahoots with that Texas Tom who tried to ambush Deputy Long in Cheyenne and got shot by Wyoming's own Marshal Casey down yonder!"

Longarm wanted to kick her. But he knew he wasn't even supposed to *kiss* her before he knew for certain he wasn't going to have to *arrest* her. She seemed a good old gal, but somebody in those parts had to be as two-faced as that Roman statue, Mr. Janus.

For his own part Longarm told the newspaperman, "I ain't accused nobody of nothing for the record, Big Jim. I understand your desire for all the news that's fit to print. But I'd be much obliged if you just held your fire, for now and, if you will, I'll give you the very first officious statement. Do we have a deal?"

Big Jim frowned thoughtfully and replied, "It sounds like a one-way marriage agreement in which I agree to love, honor, and obey you without any right to kiss you. You are so right about my having a newspaper to put out, and my readers have the right to know a hired gun is running loose in their township like a mad dog off its leash!"

Longarm snorted. "Aw, come on. I only told Miss Rita another shady character named Ram Rogers as a possible suspect. There's no solid evidence it was him and not some *other* mad dog up in the bell tower just now!"

Rita said she wanted to question this Ram Rogers whatever he was and allowed she was headed over to their J.P. to ask for a writ she could use to run the rascal in on suspicion, if nothing else, for a good seventy-two hours.

Longarm started to warn her not to swear out a felony warrant with no more to back it but the unsupported accusations of a known con man.

Then he wondered why he'd want to say a dumb thing

like that. For Billy Vail and the attorney general had asked him to find out what these Wyoming wildwomen were up to and old Rita, for all her dimples and auburn hair, was talking sort of wild right in front of him.

So he held his tongue and went along with the rest of them as they all made their way afoot down the main street and around a corner to a mansart-roofed frame house painted puke green with chocolate brown trim.

They all trooped inside to find the formidable Edith Penn Keller, J.P., presiding over her crowded parlor from a big keyhole desk set on a raised and carpet-covered dais at one end, with a gilt plaster goddess of Justice at one end and a stack of law books at the other.

The J.P., herself, was a fat lady of about forty with her dark hair drawn up in a tight bun as she sat there in black poplin judicial robes, reminding Longarm of a big black broody hen setting on a clutch of billiard balls somebody had slipped under her big ass as a joke. She was fining a young cowboy two dollars for disturbing the peace as Longarm followed Rita, two of her kid deputies, and Big Jim from the *Riverside News* in. It sounded fair to ask two dollars off a kid who'd roped and drug a watering trough the night before. But when J. P. Keller saw who'd come to admire her, or see her, least ways, she ordered everyone else to clear her court. So it wasn't clear how the case of the trough-roping cowboy would ever be resolved.

Her undersheriff introduced Longarm to the bossy older woman and Longarm found it tougher to smile at this one.

Had she been born a man, Edith Penn Keller, J.P., would have been one of those puffed-up bullfrogs who don't want anybody to tell them anything, but want to tell everybody everything.

Having been born a woman, she was one of those puffed-up cowfrogs who didn't want anybody to tell her anything but wanted to tell everybody everything. So Rita had barely explained they wanted to have Ram né Melvin Rogers brought in for questioning before the blustersome older woman declared, "Consider it done, dear heart. I'll have my law clerk type it up for you before suppertime and run it over to you. Ram Rogers aka Melvin Rogers wanted on suspicion dead or alive!"

Longarm couldn't help himself. He said, "No offense, your honor, but you can't put that on a properly made-out arrest warrant."

Edith P. scowled at him to reply, "Nonsense. I do it all the time. Didn't you just tell us the man was a hired gun who might know something about the disappearance of Deputy Ida Weaver as well as those attempts on your own life?"

Longarm said, "Yes, ma'am. I want to question him, not pay my respects at his funeral. Didn't them other federal and county lawmen tell you it ain't considered seemly to order anybody executed before they'd had a fair trial and been found guilty of a capital offense?"

She allowed she'd gotten some nitpicky letter from the district attorney over to the county seat. Then added she'd been appointed to her township position fair and square and ought to know what she was doing.

Longarm sighed and said, "You don't, if you think you can sentence a man to death on a suspicious writ. All you ladies have been lucky none of the outlaws you've sent girls after drew and fired first. For many a slick lawyer's gotten a client off on self-defense with way less documentary proof."

It was the newspaperman who asked what Longarm meant by that. The J.P. only seemed to think he was joshing.

Longarm said, "Wherever Ida Weaver is, right now, she came into a Denver saloon with the stated purpose of serving the late Rusty Mansfield with a document signed by your J. P., giving her permit to shoot him on the spot. Before that, the ladies had established that same intent by shooting other wanted men, earlier. Had Rusty Mansfield blown little Ida Weaver away, in front of me and everyone, he'd have had a pretty good excuse to present in court, and it only takes one juror to get you off if you can persuade him you had any excuse at all!''

Big Jim Tanner sighed and said, ''I fear he makes a valid point, Your Honor. As I've tried to tell you, myself, your girlish deputies would have every right to defend their own lives against known killers by shooting first and asking questions later, serving a more delicately worded legal document.''

Rita said, ''You'd better just summon Mr. Melvin Rogers to appear before you, and I'll see it's served on him, Edith.''

The J.P. asked Longarm if he had the address of the scamp.

Longarm shook his head and said, ''If I did I'd wire somebody else to pick him up, Your Honor. I want him alive and talking and there's limitations to Miss Rita's girlish approach to serving writs and warrants, no offense.''

Chapter 16

Longarm had to escort Rita back to her own place because he was a gent and because he wanted his pony and Winchester back.

Once he had them he retraced his course on horseback to the center of town and dismounted at the Western Union to send a heap of wires in every direction.

As he handed the profitable sheaf of yellow forms over to the dry and dusty-looking clerk he introduced himself and said, "I know all about the company policy laid out by your late Mr. Cornell and I hope you understand he's dead and I'm riding for the federal government, which allows you all to string considerable miles of wire over federal open range."

The clerk said, "You still don't get to read any private messages sent or received at five cents a word by this private company. I had this same conversation a few days ago with some other federal deputies out of Cheyenne."

A skinny kid with a goofy Adam's apple came in with his spurs ringing to ask where they wanted him riding next.

The clerk told him they didn't have any wires for him

to deliver. The stringbean in tight but faded denim said he'd be out front where he could admire the ladies shopping if they needed him.

As soon as they were alone again, Longarm told the clerk, "I could get me a court order if I had to, friend."

To which the clerk replied, "You have to, and don't you come at me with any writ from that fat-assed Edith Keller. For we've established how much weight she really carries with the territorial or federal courts in Cheyenne."

The old fuss didn't know he'd already answered a question Longarm had been meaning to ask somebody who knew. He smiled thinly and told the old-timer he'd noticed old Edith could lose a few pounds. But it didn't work. The Western Union man said, "Don't try to butter me up. I'm paid to be firm about company policy, and my company is not at all impressed by crossroads J.P.s of any description. Our customers pay good money for our services, and we mean to serve them right."

Longarm said, "Don't get your bowels in an uproar, old son. All I need is some delivery times and dates. The messages I suspect a local sneak has been sending and receiving are doubtless in code to begin with. But you'd have records of who got a particular wire from a particular town on a particular day, wouldn't you?"

The clerk shrugged and said, "You'd better find a judge with the weight to sway a nationwide corporation with friends in high places while I put your own messages on the wire. I know who you are, Longarm. Other clerks have reported how persuasive you can be when you want to read over their shoulders. Other clerks have gotten in a whole lot of trouble, and I told you I've already had this conversation with other lawmen. So, like the Indian chief said, I have spoken!"

He sounded like he meant it. Longarm didn't want to set his skinny jaw any firmer by arguing with him. So he paid for the wires that he couldn't send collect, and they parted as friendly as the crusty old cuss seemed to get.

Out front, that stringbean was sitting on the edge of the plank walk, ogling a gal across the way that Longarm didn't think as much of. Longarm stepped down off the walk to untether his pony as he told the kid, "I'd be U.S. Deputy Marshal Custis Long and I'm expecting a heap of answers to the wires I just sent. I'm fixing to check into the hotel across the way, and I'd be obliged if you got them to me as fast as they come in."

The kid said, "They call me Pony Bodie and I hope you understand there's a delivery charge, Deputy Long?"

Longarm nodded and said, "I never ask nobody to work for me free. I can't be traipsing back and forth betwixt the hotel and your office if I'm to get anything else done around here. So you just leave any messages at the hotel desk if I ain't in, and I'll settle up with you on your service charges when I can. I take it you're a sort of private contractor, not on the Western Union payroll?"

Pony Bodie sighed and said, "I always wanted to be a telegrapher, or mayhaps a fireman, when I grew up. But delivering wires for folk who don't want to pick 'em up at the desk inside pays better than weeding yards or beating rugs. So what the hell."

"You get to ride out to the surrounding spreads a lot?" Longarm asked as if he didn't really care.

Pony Bodie shrugged and answered, "Some. Not as often as I have to leg it here in town, though. Stockmen and homesteaders only get wires on rare and important occasions. The merchants and businessmen here at the crossing wire back and forth at a nickel a word like they had money to burn."

Longarm allowed he'd heard it cost money to make money and led old Socks across the main street afoot, not wanting to press the delivery boy too hard, this soon, within earshot of the crusty clerk inside.

At the Pronghorn Hotel across the way they told him not to be silly when he asked if he could hire a room with a bath. But at least the shitter down the hall had a modern flush tank, and they had a water tap you could use to refill the basin that went with the corner washstands in the small but fairly tidy rooms on the second floor.

They charged seventy-five cents a night for travelers laying over without riding stock. Longarm allowed a dollar a day for horse and rider sounded fair. But he followed old Socks around to their stable to make sure they knew what they were doing out back.

They did. The half-dozen other ponies they were boarding were all alive and well with a sunny corral and fresh straw bedding in the stable stalls. He left his borrowed saddle in the tack room and took the Winchester up to his hired room.

He left it leaning in a corner, took a shit down the hall, and headed next for the *Riverside News* just up the street on foot.

When he went inside he found they had a long counter cutting off the front of the twenty by forty-foot forespace from a typewriter-topped editorial desk, some filing cabinets, and a hand-cranked flatbed press in the back. Ben Franklin might have found the setup newfangled. Longarm had seen fancier.

The only individual on the premises seemed to be a gal about the right age but too pretty for that stringbean down by the Western Union. But that wasn't saying much. She was just a plain young gal with nothing wrong with her, save for a smudge of ink on one cheek. Her mousy brown hair was pinned up in a bun with a pencil shoved through it. You couldn't say much about her figure, either way, because she wore an ink smudge printer's smock of mattress ticking over whatever else she might have on.

She came over to the counter from the composing galley where she'd been sticking type, her type stick or boxlike metal holder still held in her ink-stained left hand, and got prettier as she smiled across the counter at him to ask what she could do for him.

Longarm resisted the temptation to tell her that all

depended on whether she was married-up or not. She looked sort of country for that sort of teasing. He'd been wearing his badge since he'd ridden in. So he had no call to offer her more than his name before he told her, "I'd sure like to look through your morgue, ma'am."

She looked blank and answered, "Morgue? That would be over at the county seat, Deputy Long. We have a sheriff's substation, but dead bodies are examined by the county coroner and—"

"Newspaper morgue." He cut in, explaining, "That's what they call the files of dead stories worth saving at the *Denver Post* and other such high-falutin papers. You know what airs folk put on in them bigger cities."

She brightened and said, "Oh, I think I *did* hear that term when I was working on the school paper back in Iowa. You'd better talk to Big Jim Tanner, my boss, about that. I just work here. I'm Inez Potts. They call me Inky Potts. I'm not sure just what we've been saving in yonder files. I know we don't have room to save complete back issues, and so the boss, not me, cuts out all the advertising and boiler plates."

"Boiler plates?" Longarm asked before he recalled that meant national and world-wide news supplied to small-town papers for a modest fee by the bigger news and features syndicates. They shipped what looked like boiler plates of made-up type, cast in one piece back East.

He was working on how he wanted to talk her into going behind her employer's back when Big Jim came in, puffing a cigar and looking as pleased as punch to find Longarm jawing with his hired help.

Inky went back to work as soon as she'd turned Longarm over to Big Jim, telling her boss the lawman wanted to paw through the morgue.

Big Jim said, "That's easy enough. But about us putting our heads together on a news exclusive—"

"I told you why I can't go along with you on that," Longarm cut in, trying to keep it friendly as he continued, "I don't hold my cards to my vest to cheat nobody,

135

Big Jim. I just don't want nobody cheating *me*, and I can tell you I'm dealing with a mastermind-unknown because you know he, she, or it has had me shot at from here to Cheyenne. I'll be proud to tell you all the news that's fit to print, as soon as I find out what's been going on and just who I can trust in these parts.''

"Meaning you don't trust *me*?" the burly newspaperman demanded in a tone about as warm as January in the South Pass.

Longarm smiled friendly as ever as he asked, "Is there any reason I shouldn't trust you, Big Jim?"

Tanner grimaced and said, "All right. You're going to find out in any case. I've given Rita Mae Reynolds tips on more than one owlhoot rider she had warrants out on. Before you say only a master criminal would be able to track down swaggering bully boys by Western Union, what does that make *you*? Newspapermen scattered all over the country have been comparing notes and sometimes scooping official government handouts since before the American Revolution!''

Longarm went on smiling as he said, "I read about old Sam Adams printing Patrick Henry's speeches before the Redcoats in Boston had heard he was speaking. Who told you the late Rusty Mansfield was staying at the Termont House in Denver before you told Miss Rita?"

Big Jim had his temper back under control as he calmly replied, "Let's just say I have my own confidential sources. You'll no doubt get our pretty undersheriff to tell you I have lots of confidential sources. It goes with my line, which is gathering news. If you want to be one of my confidential sources, I'll be one of your confidential sources. If you intend to treat me like an infernal suspect, see if you can get a court order violating the freedom of the press with us screaming, in headline type, on our extra editions in an election year!"

Longarm shook his his head wearily and replied, "I doubt I could manage in the time I have. But what can I tell you? You *are* a suspect. It's nothing personal. We call it the process of eliminating, and you ain't been eliminated yet.''

Big Jim snorted. ''Jesus H. Christ, do I look like the ringleader of some vast outlaw conspiracy?''

Longarm shrugged and said, ''Sheriff Henry Plummer never would have been elected if they'd known he had all them Montana Innocents riding for him. From the little I've been able to suspicion, word has been spread, by way of confidential sources, that there's easy pickings in these parts because of the local law being so . . . refined.''

He saw he'd worded that smarter when Inky Potts shot him a wary glance across the press room. Mentioning skirts around anybody in a skirt could tense things up as tight as shouting ''Greaser'' in Nuevo Laredo on a Saturday night.

Big Jim Tanner sneered, ''All right, I'll confess, I've always wanted to scoop the *Wyoming Eagle*, and nobody invited me to cover the Northfield Raid that time. So I've been trying to engineer as big a shoot-out in front of the Drover's Trust up the block! Or would you rather accuse me of luring road agents here from far and wide so's I could get them to rob somebody and then double-cross them for the loot?''

Longarm said, ''I like that better. But there's one hole in the bucket. Honor among thieves is a myth, and there's been many an old pard backshot as the robbers were fixing to divvy up the spoils. But a local boy fingering targets for outside road agents would have to gun them sooner and closer, wouldn't he?''

Big Jim nodded and said, ''Rusty Mansfield was spending the money from that stage holdup like he feared the ink would fade when . . . a certain source wired me where he'd turned up.''

''How did you know it was Rusty Mansfield as stopped the stage and shot Ida Weaver's uncle? The little I have on that one says the road agents were masked, and Rusty Mansfield was neither well known in these parts or alone.''

Big Jim said, "He was the one dumb enough to brag, once he thought he was far enough from these parts. Just like that mean drunk in the Texas Panhandle boasted of gunning that railroad worker. We're not talking about the likes of Frank and Jesse, Longarm. To begin with, they haven't all been what I'd call a professional criminal. Three or four of the nine, so far, were no more than evil-tempered brutes who killed in anger without taking a dime for their troubles. What profit would I or any other mastermind make from ordering any gunslicks to behave like that?"

Longarm said, "I was hoping you could tell me. I'd agree the whole thing was just a string of wild but unconnected incidents if Deputy Ida Weaver wasn't missing and nobody seemed to be shooting at me, personal. It all started late last winter with Amarillo Cordwain gunning that Irish railroad man, right?"

Big Jim nodded, started to say something, then laughed like hell and called out to his type sticker, "Will you listen to this slick talker, Inky? You just heard me telling him we won't play ball with him unless he's willing to play ball with us, and here I am playing ball with him!"

Then he said, "Get out of here, Longarm. I have a paper to publish, and we work together my way or we don't work together at all!"

Chapter 17

The workday was winding down by then. But Longarm had time to do some eliminating that Billy Vail would have applauded. For in a town that small and close-knit it was easy to eliminate like hell with casual questions about who'd been doing what with whom when what was going on.

He'd known right off that neither he, Rita Mae, nor her household help had been smoking up her front parlor with that old army rifle from the bell tower. It hardly made sense that Preacher Shearer would have had to bust his own locked door to get into his own church and the notion of the sniper busting in before dawn when nobody was on the streets of Keller's Crossing eliminated heaps of others.

For everybody with a regular job near the center of town had been at work instead of up in that bell tower and had plenty of others to back their alibi. *Alibi* came from a Latin term meaning ''somewheres else,'' and it was tough to fathom how anybody could be lying in ambush up among the pigeons and going about their usual chores in front of everybody.

The very few who were too important to be laboring

in public, such as that snotty newspaper man, the preacher himself, and most of the public officials of Keller's Crossing had all come running from the wherevers they'd been in response to the gunshots later in the day. So whilst it burned like fire, Longarm had to allow those rifle shots had been fired by somebody who was neither holding a steady job near that church nor a total stranger to those who did. It had to be at least a face they'd seen before. Folk remembered strange faces in small towns, whether they'd done anything or not. Many a horse thief had learned this to his cost when the local vigilance committee rode him down after he thought he'd gotten away clean from a town where nobody was supposed to know he was a horse thief.

As he headed back to his hotel to see if they served supper Longarm reflected that eliminating most everyone he'd met in Keller's Crossing as that sniper didn't mean he, she, or it hadn't been carrying out the orders of somebody more two-faced. He didn't see how he was going to eliminate anyone as the mastermind who'd almost surely done something to that Deputy Ida Weaver and been trying to do something to him ever since he'd talked to the deadly but not-too-bright little gal.

As he approached the hotel, he spied Pony Bodie and another young buckaroo drooling at the passing womenfolk out front of the Western Union. Pony Bodie saw him and got up to lope over, calling out he'd just delivered a wire from Denver to the desk clerk inside.

Longarm reached in his jeans for a silver dollar and handed it over, saying, "Keep the change. How would you like to make a little more on the side?"

Pony Boyle looked wary and said, "Lord knows I could use some. But I ain't one for any queer stuff if that's what we're talking about."

Longarm assured him that wasn't what they were talking about as he tore a sheet out of his notebook that he'd already made some notes on. Handing it to the delivery boy, Longarm said, "I don't need to read any private telegraph messages that are likely in code to begin with.

140

You'll find just some dates and the names of other towns on this page. I need to know who got a wire here in this township on let's say more than three or four of them dates, and from where.''

Pony Bodie took the slip of paper but pointed out, ''I generally deliver telegrams to all sorts of folk every day in the week.''

Longarm said, ''You weren't listening. We call it a process of eliminating when one particular address gets more wires than anybody else from particular parts of this vast country, see?''

Pony Boyle grinned and said, ''I reckon I do, now. Maybe I'll be a lawman instead of a telegrapher when I grow up. I dasn't poke about in files until old Wilbur leaves for the night. You just talked to him, and you should have seen what a prune he is. I get along better with the night man, Herb. I fetch sandwiches and suds for him after dark, and in return he's been showing me how to send dots and dashes when things get slow. He's even let me send night letters when nobody else was around. I reckon I can check these dates out for you, later, after I've fetched him them suds.''

They shook on it and Longarm went on in to pick up his wire from Billy Vail and ask about supper. They served plain-and-simple off the taproom grill. So he ordered a T-bone with home-fries and forget the damned turnip greens. He read the wire from his boss as he waited to be served. Vail wasn't able to tell him anything he didn't already know. But old Billy agreed that a missing witness and repeated attempts to stop a totally ignorant lawman meant they were likely worried little Ida Weaver might have given something away. Billy agreed that if the gal was still alive, she'd have been able to convince them by this time that she hadn't. He wanted to know if Longarm had the least notion who might be holding Ida Weaver, or her body, where. It was sort of comforting to see that even a paid-up U.S. marshal could ask dumb questions.

He topped off his supper with serviceberry pie and

went easy on the coffee because he'd had a long hard day, likely face another one, and a man had to sleep now and again, even alone in a strange bed.

He went over to the tobacco shop near the railroad platform to buy some bed-reading and make sure he had the time table on that line right. Then he headed back to his hotel as the sun was setting, sort of glad they'd shut down all the rowdy saloons in town because it was easier to turn in early when everybody else had to.

But when he got upstairs with his new edition of *Police Gazette*, he spied a match stem on the floor when no match stem was supposed to be unless some sneaky son of a bitch had opened his hired door while he was going about more honest chores!

He had the key to the damned door in his jacket pocket. Before trying it in the lock, he cautiously twisted the knob to see if the door was locked. He found it wasn't. So he flung it open to dive through and roll across the rug with his six-gun drawn and the pink pages of the scattered *Police Gazette* fluttering in every direction.

He kicked the door shut behind him with a bootheel as he yelled, "Freeze, you mother, and I don't mean mother dear!"

"Custis, is that you?" a surprised familiar voice called back.

Longarm was surprised, too, as he stared up at the womanly outline seated on his bed against the gloaming light from the window to reply, "What in thunder are you doing up this way, Miss Covina? I never sent for young Daisy yet!"

The widow woman said, "Thanks for reminding me I'm not young. I thought you'd want your derringer back, and you can't send for young Daisy. She seems to have been born restless. I'd have worried about a kidnapping if she hadn't cleaned out the till while I thought she was tending shop for me."

Longarm got up and put his gun away with a sheepish grin as he said, "I'll see if I can get my outfit to make

142

up your losses for you, Miss Covina. I knew right off she was a tramp. But I thought she was too smart to bite hands that were feeding her that well, and I needed her help up this way.''

He tossed his Stetson on the nearby dresser and began to pick up the scattered pink pages as Covina replied, ''Wasn't that just like a man to put all his eggs in such a trashy basket? I thought that I'd better warn you she was gone before you sent for her. So I caught the noon combination, and I've been here a while. I didn't think you'd want me to tell them we were plotting something when I checked in downstairs. Would you care to tell me what we're plotting now?''

He could see her better as he tidied up closer to the window with the light coming over his own shoulder. She was wearing a silk brocade kimono with green and gold dragons crawling all over the black background. It was open enough at the top to prove what Ben Franklin had written about women and trees withering from the top. Her sweet face wasn't all that wrinkled, despite the mop of steel-wire hair.

He said, ''I see you left your travel duster and other baggage in your own room. How did you get in here without a key, Miss Covina?''

She demurely replied, ''The door wasn't locked. When I knocked and nobody answered, I tried the door and found it opened. So I assumed you'd be back soon, and here I've been sitting for what seems like a mighty long time. Do I get to hear the big secret now?''

Longarm grimaced and moved over to the saddlebags he'd brought up from the tack room. As he went throught them, he confided, ''The one who picked that lock left me all my spare socks and such. I reckon he, she, or it was after the papers I've been packing on me, personal. Are you sure nobody downstairs knows you're in here with me?''

She said, ''I don't see who could have told them. I never mentioned you when I told them I was up this way from Cheyenne on business and couldn't say how long I might be here. How long might I be here, you secretive thing?''

Longarm moved over to the door again and threw the bolt as he told her, ''Ain't sure. We're waiting on a tip about another secretive cuss. I'll be mighty surprised if somebody doesn't suddenly tell Undersheriff Reynolds where Ram Rogers has run off to.''

Covina Rivers sighed and said, ''I saw you and that other man talking to her up the street from my own window, earlier. I asked a chambermaid who that glamorous young thing might be. I can see why you men are so interested in her. What does that female judge look like?''

Longarm knew better than to describe Edith Penn Keller, J.P., as anything worse than fat and opinionated. The old but nicely built shopkeeper sniffed and said, ''Poor thing. According to our Daisy, you only seem to go for the young and inexperienced ones.''

Longarm laughed incredulously and replied, ''I'd hardy call Daisy inexperienced. But if she told you I'd been messing with her, she was a bare-faced liar. I ain't no innocent schoolboy, and I'll allow she was tempting. But I wanted her to help me catch crooks more than I wanted to play slap and tickle with her, bless her devious hide.''

Covina leaned back on her elbows, one bare knee peeping out at him through the folds of her silk kimono as she calmly asked, ''Does that mean we get to play slap and tickle after I help you catch some crooks?''

Longarm gulped as he considered his options. Then, seeing he was as damned if he didn't as he'd be damned if he did, he decided he'd as soon cuss himself in the morning for acting natural than cuss himself for sending her away mad.

But as he flopped across the pillow beside her, the widow gal, being a gal, gasped, ''Custis! Can't you take a little teasing?''

To which he could only reply, taking her tenderly but firmly in his arms, ''I reckon we've teased each other long enough. If the two of us are going to work as a team, we'd best get this bullshit out of the way.''

"Oh, Custis, you're so romantic!'' She giggled as he ran his free hand inside her kimono to discover, as he kissed her, she was built as girlish as that sneaky little Daisy or even Inky Potts at the *Riverside News*. But picturing little Inky in this same position, with his hand inside a printer's smock instead of a kimono, inspired him to slide said hand down Covina's trembling bare flesh to part the thatch betwixt her thighs without considering how gray it might be while she tried to cross her legs, muttering, ''No! Not yet! It's been so long, and I have to get used to the idea and . . .'' But he'd whipped it out and rolled atop her in his duds to let nature take its course, and as it did so Covina sobbed, ''Oh, my lands, it *is* so long and a girl could sure get used to this! But don't you want to take your clothes off, darling?''

He said he sure did. But she had to help him some, and he still had his jeans down around his booted ankles when they came, and then came some more, as only a healthy young man who hadn't had any the night before and a sweet little old lady who hadn't had any for even longer could manage, sobbing in mutual sincere ecstacy.

"Oh, thank you, thank you, *thank* you!'' the shop-keeper sobbed as he lay limp betwixt her surprisingly springy thighs, letting it soak in her as her warm wet innards pulsed around it.

He began to move his hips experimentally as he got his breath back and said, conversationally, ''It ain't that I'd be ashamed to be seen in public with you, Miss Covina. But it's important we keep it a secret that we've met before, see?''

She thrust her pelvis up to him as she replied just as calmly that she'd already assumed that much.

Then she marveled, ''Are you really doing what it feels like you're doing down there, you naughty boy? Didn't I satisfy you, just now?''

He kissed her some more and said, ''You purely did and I hope you felt that grand a gallop up amongst the stars, Miss Covina. But if it's all the same with you, I'd like to satisfy us both again.''

She moaned that nothing would please her more and got to weeping and laughing at the same time when he hooked an elbow under either of her knees to spread her wide for some long-donging as she protested that she'd never taken it that deep before, then begged him not to stop when he eased back enough to keep from hitting bottom with every probing stroke. He suspected he was teaching her what a lot of gals went to their graves without ever learning. Gals tended to be as bossy as their man would let them be. So a heap of otherwise loving couples never got down and dirty because women never admitted they liked it that way. Old Covina swore at him and told him her late husband had never rutted with her half so cruel. But when he growled he didn't want nobody else in bed with them that evening, she giggled and told him her late husband had been a dear, but not near as much of a natural man. Then they were both too busy to talk for a spell.

Later, as they lay still in the gathering darkness, sharing one of his cheroots, Longarm patted her bare shoulder and said, ''I reckon I ought to tell you what the plan is now.''

But Covina asked, ''Can't it wait, darling? I don't know what's gotten into me tonight but I'm still throbbing like a tabby cat in heat and . . . Would you mind if I sucked you hard again and got on top this time?''

He lay back, legs ajar with the cheroot gripped in his grinning teeth as he told her, ''Suit yourself, old pal. But whilst you're at it, here's my plan. . . .''

Chapter 18

Covina crept back to her own room in the wee small hours lest the hotel help give the show away. Longarm slept later than usual for some reason but finally decided there was no fun lying slugabed when there was no office to report in late to.

So Longarm was having eggs over hash for breakfast in the taproom downstairs when Pony Bodie caught up with him, packing a sheaf of sealed telegrams and a handwritten list on brown paper.

Longarm invited the youth to set and coffee up as he shoved the wires in a hip pocket for later and spread the list on the table beside his own mug.

Pony Bodie said, "I ought to charge you and Western Union overtime. I had to hang around last night until old Herb dozed off in his chair before I snuck into the shithouse with a file drawer. Figuring out what I was doing was a bitch, too. But as I pawed through the delivery slips with your own list in hand, I commenced to see what you meant."

Longarm said they called it a "pattern" in his line of work as he sipped coffee and perused the childish scrawls.

He saw a pattern right off. Pony Bodie had only listed the names of locals getting wires from certain places on certain dates. So most of the names, including Big Jim Tanner, had no more than one or two listings under them. But Preacher Shearer, or at least his manse, had nine that fit like gloves and one left over.

Longarm cocked a brow and observed, "I see you delivered a wire from Pueblo, Colorado, just yesterday."

As the breed waitress put his coffee down in front of him, Pony Bodie said, "Sure I did. You asked me to make up that list long after. I don't know who sent it or what it said because they give me the telegrams sealed. I run it up to the manse early in the day. Way before somebody shot out Miss Rita's bay window. I don't know nothing about that, neither."

Longarm smiled thinly and said, "I know. I asked where you were at the time. You and some pals were spitting and whittling across the street when them shots rang out."

Pony Bodie blinked owlishly at him and said, "I'm sure glad I ain't out to steal that handsome buckskin you rode in on. I don't know who might have been up in that bell tower or how come Preacher Shearer got all them wires from all over. Why don't you ask him?"

Longarm said, "I mean to. Soon as I finish my breakfast."

The kid wanted to tag along. But Longarm told him not to and added, "I'd be obliged if you refrained from repeating this conversation to anybody else. Anybody else at all. *Comprende?*"

Pony Bodie gulped and allowed he did, sort of. So they strode out in the morning sunlight together and parted friendly.

You had to pass the *Riverside News* before you got to the church in any case. So Longarm stepped inside to find little Inky Potts sticking type in the back, alone. Her hips looked a tad less full than he'd pictured them the night before, going dog style with old Covina.

When she came to the counter with a wary smile on

148

her ink-smudged face, Longarm said, "I'll get right to
the point, Miss Inky. Your boss and me don't get along
as well as I'd like. He may be innocent of any other
crime, or you could be working for a killer. I need your
help in finding out. You look smart enough to see it's
in your own best interests to help me find out, either
way. Your turn."

She gasped. "Oh, dear Lord, I knew being paid a
man's wages with nobody trying to get up my skirt was
too good to be true! If you had any idea what a girl goes
through in the newspaper game!"

He said, "I do. Some of my best friends are newspaper gals. But I never asked about Big Jim's employ-
ment policies. He won't let me go through your morgue.
I'd be able to tell you why, a heap better, if you were
to go through it for me and answer the few simple questions I've put down on this one page from my notebook."

She took the tightly lettered list warily and said she
couldn't promise anything. He said, "I ain't asking for
promises. I just need some answers. Before you go running with this to Big Jim, be advised I've already caught
him in one lie. I'm still working on whether that means
he's a self-important small-town big shot or a dangerous
felon. So, for your own protection, slip the answers to
me discreet as you know how as soon as you can manage."

She said she'd try but made no promises. Longarm
had noticed the ones who hesitated to promise you the
moon were most likely to show up with something.

He left the newspaper just in time. Big Jim in the
beefy flesh was coming down the walk. As they met,
the newspaperman asked if Longarm had any scoops for
him. Longarm replied it was too early to say and started
to move on. Big Jim told him the good looking undersheriff was down the other way, in her substation.

Longarm asked what had made the newspaperman
think he was on his way to pester Miss Rita. Big Jim
laughed and said, "Come on, I got a darkie keeping

149

house for me, too, and you know how they gossip.''

''Almost as bad as the rest of us,'' Longarm conceded in a disgusted tone before he suggested, ''Tell your darkie to tell Miss Rita's darkie that the lady of the house received me in her front parlor on officious business with her hair pinned up.''

To say they parted friendly would have been a fib. Longarm legged it on up to the church and knocked on the front door of the adjoining manse until he got tired of that and went around to knock on the back door.

Nobody came. There should have been at least a cleaning woman in charge if the preacher was out saving souls or sending sneaky wires.

Longarm started to go around the front to see if the older man was in the church, itself. Then he had a better idea and moved around to the back to find that, sure enough, there was a gap left in the hedge with just such a shortcut in mind.

Longarm followed the visible path in the yardgrass to a cellar door at the rear of the bigger frame church. It wasn't padlocked. A man of the cloth who ran back and forth a lot likely figured nobody else would notice a celler door in the shady gap between the church and manse. Longarm could see nobody had any way of watching him as he drew his .44-40 and pulled one leaf of the door up with his free hand.

It was dark and musty at the bottom of the brick stairs. Longarm eased down them, reminded of that old song that went

Oh the deacon went down
To the cellar to pray.
And he found a little jug,
and he stayed all day!

But there was nothing to be seen or smelled except spiderwebs and, over on a far wall, some chalk drawings on the dark damp bricks.

Longarm moved closer and the right realistic drawing

looked even dirtier. He whistled under his breath as he perused the pornographic pictures of male figures in some of the damnedest positions. None of them appealed to a man who admired women way more than shapeless men with impossible peckers and seeingly bottomless assholes.

He moved over to another flight of steps on the balls of his feet, wondering who might have drawn such dirty pictures in the cellar of a church without anybody noticing.

He eased up the steps to a closed door that might lead out to anywheres. But as he cracked it open with his own asshole puckered, he saw he seemed to be behind the altar and that made sense for the gents most likely to sneak into church this way.

Longarm moved around the high-back screen of the altar to see who else might be in church at that hour of the morning. He saw a hulking figure kneeling in a pew closer to the front door, facing the other way because he didn't seem to be praying with that pistol of his own trained on said front door!

Longarm braced his right elbow on the corner of the altar to train the muzzle of his own six-gun steady as he stated in a firm but not unkindly tone, "I got the drop on you, Bergman. Before you turn around, I want you to lay that pistol down and—"

The Black Swede spun around to fire a wild shot that was sure to throw the pipe organ out of tune. So Longarm fired before the crazy son of a bitch could figure out what he wanted to shoot at.

The big and doubtless crazy brake bull reeled but crabbed sideways out of that pew, shaking his head like an angry bull in the haze of his own gunsmoke as he screamed awful things in Swedish and fired yet another shot, into the floor between them, as Longarm blazed away to stagger him backward with six hundred grains of hot lead in him.

Gus Bergman crashed against the recently repaired front door and busted it wide open to land face up on the front steps with a peaceful expression on his ugly face at last.

Longarm strode out into the sunlight to stand over him, reloading, as he muttered, "Jesus H. Christ. How are you going to tell me what's been going on *now*? Didn't they ever tell you confession was good for the soul? With you dead, you son of a bitch, I'm staring at the damnedest run of pure coincidence or a plot that would cross old Machiavelli's eyes!"

By this time the whole town had come running in response to the gunplay, of course. Big Jim Tanner was first on the scene with Rita Mae Reynolds and two of her kid deputies close behind.

Longarm ignored the newspaperman's questions as the undersheriff stared down at the mess at his feet to exclaim, "I know him on sight. He works for the railroad, and we asked them to switch him to another line when he kept getting into fights. I think his name was Bergen."

Longarm said, "Bergman. I've tangled with him more recent. He was working on another spur line, and I'll be switched with snakes if I can see how anyone knew I'd be riding north that way instead of this way. I know they were watching for me around the Cheyenne railyards. But I met up with this homicidal maniac before I ever got to Cheyenne!"

Somebody in the crowd thought to ask if Preacher Shearer was all right. Longarm said he'd been next door, and there didn't seem to be anybody home.

Rita said, "There's always somebody there. Preacher Shearer has an old Indian squaw keeping house for him. We'd better find out why nobody came to the door!"

They did. Longarm said nothing about search warrants as the law that worked there forced the lock of the back door. They found the plump brown corpse of the middle-aged housekeeper faceup on the kitchen floor without a stitch of clothing on. Her throat had been slit from ear to ear. It was the shemale undersheriff who allowed right out that they'd have the county coroner determine what other crimes had been committed on or about her.

Longarm led the way forward through the house that smelled of blood and crud. He found Preacher Shearer's naked body in a front office, facedown amid blood-spattered books and papers, with a corncob shoved up his ass and a pigging-string knotted tight around his wrists. He'd been stabbed, a heap, with what looked like a Malay kris but was likely a paper knife. It was still in him, betwixt the shoulder blades.

Longarm moved quickly to the door and tried to stop Rita from entering as he tersely told her, "You're right. We'd best wait on the coroner's report, Miss Rita."

She tried to walk through him, demanding, "What happened? Why won't you let me see?"

He said, "What happened looks like the last act of Hamlet directed by the Marquis de Sade. I don't want you to see in yonder because you really don't *want* to see in yonder."

But she insisted and she was the law with two deputies backing her. So Longarm stood aside and braced himself to hear some screaming.

But old Rita took it like a man, or at least a lady undersheriff who took her job serious, and moved in to scout for sign, being as careful as Longarm about where she planted her feet. It was she who noticed the yellow telegram in a far corner and moved over to hunker down and read it.

Once she had, she stared up at Longarm to say, "Somebody signing his or her name *Horny* sent this message from Pueblo, Colorado, to this poor dead preacher man, of all people! It says plain as day that their mutual friend Ram Rogers just checked in to the Black Diamond Hotel near the depot. I don't understand this at all!"

From the doorway Big Jim Tanner said, "I think I might. I told you we print all the news that's fit to print. When they pay you to be nosy, you hear things you dare not print. Some say the preacher, there, liked young men. A lot. Young men who've spent much time in

153

prison or hiding out together in lonely cabins tend to learn the same bad habits.''

Longarm quietly said, ''You told me you'd been tipping off Miss Rita to the whereabouts of wanted outlaws by comparing notes with other newspapermen. I happen to know you never got wire one about half a dozen of the rascals.''

Big Jim smiled sheepishly and said, ''I was coming to that. That poor twisted sister on the floor was my informant. Like a newspaperman, a preacher hears all sorts of gossip, even when he's not, ah, entertaining young saddle tramps and riders of the Owlhoot Trail.''

Longarm whistled low and said, ''In sum, he was nibbling on bad apples, and you were blackmailing him.''

That had been a statement rather than a question. But Big Jim blustered, ''The hell you say! Sorry, Miss Rita. Preacher Shearer was the one who approached me. He never said anything about being queer, and I never let on I knew. He only told me he'd heard the law was after such and such a wayward youth and thought he ought to pass on some gossip he'd heard from poor but more honest cowboys.''

Rita was the one who decided, ''I'm sorry I just felt sorry for the old two-faced sodomite! I see it all now! He wasn't a criminal mastermind double-crossing his followers for the loot! He was offering a hideout to like-minded outlaws passing through, then turning them in to us to shut them up forever about his depraved secret life!''

Longarm shrugged and said, ''Some of the earlier ones might have liked gals. But he'd have surely noticed, the same as the rest of us, how fatal it could be to be wanted by the law in these parts!''

Rita dimpled up at him to reply, ''You heard me tell Edith I meant to take Ram Rogers alive. As a matter of fact, I have just the deputy for the task. She and I were just talking about that very villain at my substation. She came up from Cheyenne to complain he'd run off with her shop girl and the contents of her till. Her name is

Covina Rivers, and I'd just told her we didn't know
where he was when we heard all that gunplay. Come
on. I'll introduce you to her while my boys tidy up
around here!''

Chapter 19

Miss Sarah Bernhardt could not have been a greater actress, nor the Baron Münchhausen a bigger liar as Longarm shook with the lady he'd spent most of the night before with in the sheriff's substation near the crossing. The Wyoming widow woman with a grudge against the wanted man who'd robbed her was smart enough just to look dumb when Rita said, a ways into their conversation, "I don't understand how a womanizing rascal who ran off with that young girl who worked for you could have been mixed up with a bunch of swishy boys."

Longarm soothed, "I can. I deal with heaps of crooks who spend as much time behind bars as out pestering women. Most of them tend to part their hair on both sides unless they mean to spend half their lives just admiring themselves, if you follow my drift."

Rita blushed and told him he was awful while Covina pretended not to understand.

She had to catch the early combination south unless she meant to wait all day for the passenger varnish to roll in and back out. Longarm excused himself well ahead of time so's the two of them could enjoy some girlish talk. He'd already instructed Covina how to wire him in code from Cheyenne, using another name, and let him know whether they'd told her to simper up to Ram Rogers and throw down at him to take him thudergasted but alive, or simply shoot him down like a dog.

He went out on the street and headed back toward the church, where most everyone else in town was still gathered.

When he got as far as the newspaper office, he turned in to see how Inky Potts felt about their earlier conversation.

She came right over to the counter, type stick in hand, to sort of whisper, even though they were alone, "I just heard some railroad man murdered Preacher Shearer and his squaw and that you'd shot it out with their killer! Is that true?"

Longarm said, "I ain't sure. I got the distinct impression Bergman was waiting for me in the church next door, with a gun. The preacher and his housekeeper were killed with a big fancy knife. After that I can't figure out how anybody connected with anybody could have known I was going to bum a ride up from Denver aboard a rattler Gus Bergman had already been assigned to police. There was a lady involved as well, and I just can't for the life of me figure out how my meeting up with her could have been ... Hold on! I just remembered something. She wasn't aboard the train when I got on. She came aboard *after* me! If they had her trailing me ... Lord have mercy if a man can't get his brain cells stampeding in every direction if he fails to ride herd on 'em! Have you had time to dig through the morgue for me yet?"

Inky gulped and murmured, "No. I'm paid to *work* here. But I've been over your list of questions, and they don't look too hard to answer, if you'd care to tell me what sense they make."

He said, "I don't have time to read all the fine print on each and every issue of the *Riverside News* going all the way back to the last election. So I've asked you to

158

dig out just the columns that might answer what we call key questions. I need them recent obituaries more than anything else, if you're pressed for time."

She hesitated.

He said, "*I'm* pressed for time, too, Miss Inky. I like to strike when the iron is hot, and the iron could be cooling a heap, even as we talk."

She reached in a pocket of her smock for a note she'd obviously composed ahead of time and gave it to him, murmuring, "Come to this address at high noon. Mr. Tanner has ordered me, directly, not to tell you anything about the way he may choose to run his own newspaper, on pain of instant unemployment. But we are talking about *murder*, and I guess a girl has the right to see who she wants during her own lunch hour, as long as her boss never finds out!"

So Longarm put the slip of paper away and left looking innocent. He got back to the church to find the crowd even bigger. He saw Pony Bodie and some others there, wearing guns in spite of the city ordinance passed by the ladies who ran the same.

He asked how come and Pony Bodie said, "We're fixing to posse up. Didn't you know somebody murdered the preacher and his old squaw? I just heard you were there. Wasn't that you as shot the railroad man they just carried over to the undertaker's root celler?"

Longarm said, "You heard right about me. You're the second one who called that fat housekeeper a squaw. She'd have preferred *weya* if she was Lakota. I take it you all mean squaw in the sense of an unofficious but cozy situation?"

The beanpole snickered and said, "Everybody knew how cozy they was. I mean, sure, nobody ever caught them in the act. But what else would a preacher man with no wife or lady friends be doing with a squaw sharing his bed and board?"

Longarm suggested the poor old gal might have been dusting the furniture and cooking his meals for him when they weren't tearing at each other's duds. Then he went inside to jaw with more sensible young gents.

Nobody had uncovered any new evidence in the manse. But by then they'd of course discovered the dirty drawings and some amazing devices made of India rubber in the celler under the church. Longarm agreed it was sort of shocking to picture prim and proper churchgoers singing hymns upstairs whilst double-gaited owlhoot riders were carrying on so wild right under them.

Longarm said he'd read about Canaanites in olden times who'd run a whorehouse smack in their temple, recruiting wives and daughters of their parish to whore with strangers for temple offerings.

The deputy he told this to said he'd always wondered how come the Lord had favored the Children of Israel over them dad-blasted Canaanites.

Longarm consulted his pocket watch as he considered all the mean things folk were capable of around churches. He saw it was going on eleven-thirty and allowed he had other chores to tend.

One involved some straight draft and a ham and cheese on rye before he decided it was safe to slip away from the center of town while so many others were busy eating.

Inky Potts seemed to live above a carriage house in cramped but private quarters up under the shingles. When she let him in, he saw she'd washed her hands and face, albeit there was still printer's ink under her nails, and she'd changed into a calico pinafore or had it on all the time under that shapeless smock.

Her shape was mighty handsome in calico with her waist cinched in like so. He didn't ask why her mousy brown but luxurious hair hung down her back to her shapely derriere. He thought it was just as well she had a job that kept her on her feet more than most women when he saw she meant to serve glazed doughnuts with chocolate milk.

As she carried the tray over, she indicated where he was to sit on the edge of a made-up cot and said, "Take off your jacket and gun, at least, and try to look guilty if anyone bursts in on us. I'd rather have Mr. Tanner think we were secret lovers than have him fire me for going against his orders!''

Longarm asked who was most likely to bust in on them as he shucked his jacket and gun belt to hang them up with his hat.

Inky said, ''You wouldn't be here if I really expected to be caught with you. But a girl has to plan ahead if she means to make her way in a man's world.''

Longarm told her she reminded him of a hobo gal he'd been talking to about conditions there in Wyoming Territory. As he sat down on the cot beside her, she started going into Women's Suffrage being a snare and a delusion. But he cut her off with, ''I could have told you how much fun it is to bring home the bacon, Lord willing and the creeks don't rise. But that ain't what I come for, no offense. Did you get me those obituaries, at least?''

She pressed glazed doughnuts and a tall glass of chocolate milk on him as she replied, ''That was easy. We enjoy a healthy climate here in Wyoming Territory, and no more than four local residents have died at all, and only one has been buried in that churchyard across from the undersheriff's house.''

She inhaled some doughnut and chocolate milk while he was asking her who they might be talking about.

She said, ''Mr. Nathan Hemmings, age seventy-two, with hog farming as his main occupation and pneumonia listed as the cause of death. I know it's been warm since the middle of May, but he caught a case of walking pneumonia last winter and couldn't seem to shake it before it killed him just before the Fourth of July. Is there any point to all this, Deputy Long?''

Longarm said, ''Call me Custis, seeing we're secret lovers. The point may be that our hog farmer ain't been in his grave as long as most in yonder churchyard. By dying so recent he missed the spring thaw entire.''

She pondered his words, grimaced, and said, ''Please,

ah, Custis, not while I'm *eating*! I know they embalmed him and all, but he's been down there long enough to . . . You don't suspect he's *not* down there, do you?''

Longarm chuckled and told her, ''That's about the only notion I've yet to consider. I'll take your word we're talking about an elderly victim of walking pneumonia who never murdered nobody and vice versa.''

She said she'd brought the one tally of election results he'd asked for, adding it had been deep in the files where she doubted anybody else would ever look. He said he'd read it later. Then he took a deep breath and told her, ''Miss Inky, you've been a big help and I know you don't owe me more. But I don't know who else to turn to. I know it's asking way more of you than I should. But I don't know any other gal in town I could ask, so—''

Then he noticed her hand was in his lap as she sighed and said, ''You men are all alike, thank heavens. I know you've been here overnight with nobody else to turn to, thanks to our reform administration. But, honestly, can't you silly boys go more than a night or so without any? We girls do it all the time!''

Longarm gulped and declared, ''That well may be. But I've noticed you shy violets seem to make up for lost time when you *do* get worked up!''

She giggled and said, ''We're always worked up. We just don't get to show it as often or as openly as you fresh things!''

Then she had his dick out, hard, as she slid off the cot to her knees on the rug, adding, ''A girl with a reputation and other unwanted results to worry about learns to bide her time. We're stronger than you men. I've been here in Wyoming since last summer, and this is the first chance I've had, thanks to that old fuss I work for!''

Then she lowered her pretty face to his lap to wet her lush lips and proceed to give him a French lesson that would have cost a week's pay in New Orleans!

As he stiffened in pleasure, surprised at how hard she had him after all that time in old Covina's experienced

162

flesh, Longarm moaned, "Let's get undressed and do it right! I don't want to come this way, you pretty little thing!"

She stopped sucking long enough to grin up at him like a mean little kid and said, "Later. After I get off work this evening. Right now we don't have time for a proper orgy. So let's come fast as well as wicked. You'll never guess what I'm doing to myself down here while I'm sucking you off up there!"

Then she couldn't talk with her mouth full, and he didn't much care what was going on in her ring-dang-doo if it couldn't be with his old organ-grinder. Then he was coming, and, as always, it was driving him wild with mingled desires to be in every possible position at once as she took it all the way down her throat with her tongue licking the balls she'd pulled out of his jeans.

Then, as abruptly as she'd started, Inky Potts withdrew her smiling face from his lap, saying, "That's enough, for now. I have to get back to my job while I still have one!"

He could only lay there with his dick hanging out as he watched her tidy herself up, cool as if she'd just gotten up after a night alone.

As she brushed and pinned up her long hair, seated beside him on the cot, Longarm saw the red wax candle she'd left on the rug between his boots had been rounded off and molded sort of sassy at the thick end. He took some comfort in the modest dimensions of the candle she seemed to know better than him. He'd read somewhere that both men and women who took to using dildos or substitutes for the real thing tended to work their way up to bigger and bigger insertions until a real dick wasn't nearly enough to satisfy them.

She caught the direction of his interest and flushed slightly to confess, "I told you I've been doing without for months. I'm only a woman, not a saint or the kid sister Mr. Tanner seems to take me for."

Longarm said, "I thought I heard you say a wandering printer gal has to worry about men trying to get under her skirts.''

To which she replied, ''It all depends on who might be trying to do so, when. You men have the strangest sense of time and place. How would you like it if some girl made a grab for your buttocks when you were bending over to pick up an anvil?''

Longarm chuckled and said, ''A heap of anvils would no doubt be dropped on heaps of toes. I'm glad you thought this was the time to grab my dick, Miss Inky. But that wasn't the favor I was about to ask of you.''

She said, ''I know. I told you you'd have to wait until I came home from work if you wanted to go all the way with me. That is what you really wanted, and I will find you here when I get back, won't I?''

Longarm's dick was soft enough to put away for the time being as he assured her he'd stay right where he was. So she kissed him, said she couldn't wait for closing time, and told him to help himself to anything else she had to offer before she lit out on him.

So Longarm never had to tell her that was what he'd been meaning to ask if he could do. He needed a place to hide out in Keller's Crossing while he let his plot with good old Covina take shape. You didn't have to lie to folks when they didn't see you and might even think you'd left town, satisfied.

So Longarm took off his duds and got into Inky's bed to read the telegrams and news clippings while he waited for her to come back and give him some real satisfaction.

Chapter 20

Inky did. It was just as well he'd had a whole afternoon's rest and heaps of sugar and chocolate to keep him going, once Inky had cooked him a fine supper and undressed entire for dessert.

It was purely a marvel, he thought, as he mounted the sweet young thing with two pillows under her firm little ass, how different gals could get and still seem lovely with two pillows under their asses.

For Covina had been a pale-thighed novelty after Lakota Sue, and the frolicksome fullblood had been nothing like the more sedate-looking but just as passionate Portia Parkhurst, attorney-at-law. He decided Inky reminded him more of that young wagon train gal from Poland, save for having different-colored hair, no Polish accent, and, come to study on it, a different way of moving her ass. It was only her ass that reminded him of that other sweet kid from Poland.

She took it dog style more like good old Roping Sally, save for Inky being built way smaller and good old Roping Sally being dead.

Thinking of dead gals reminded him of that Deputy Ida Weaver who'd shot Rusty Mansfield in front of him down in Denver. Looking down at a dead gal in this position would be awful, but he couldn't help wondering what he'd missed by treating her with so much respect. The poor thing might have still been alive, taking it dog style, had not he been ordered to tail her at such a discreet distance.

When Inky got on top with the late sun painting tiger stripes of light and shadow through the blinds on her pale bouncing body, she didn't do it at all like old Covina, and he was glad. He'd be meeting up with old Covina in a day or so, and it would be as bad as being married up if all the gals a man went to bed with screwed the same.

Inky fucked him all the different ways she could think of, and, as the old trail song went, if she'd have had wings she'd have fucked him flying. But they had plenty of time to smoke, talk, and even catch up on their sleep before she was shaking him awake by his dick and demanding he tell her where the night had flown.

He said he didn't know how high up went or how long forever was, either. So they tore off a morning quickie, had bacon and eggs, and she left first, warning him to be discreet, as she put it, when he let himself out.

Longarm tried to be. He waited until nigh nine, when everyone would be at work, and slipped out and along a shady alley, fully dressed, to circle around to the vomit-green house of old Edith Penn Keller, J.P.

He found the black-robed fat lady telling a young boy she couldn't issue him a wedding license no matter how much he loved the little gal next door. When it was Longarm's turn, he said he'd come for a writ of exhumation. He had to explain that was a permit to open a grave. One got the impression their J.P. had never attended Harvard Law.

She said it was jake with her if he wanted to dig a hog farmer up. She rang for her clerk, a little brown sparrow, and told Longarm to just spell out what he needed.

So Longarm did and a few minutes later he was over at the churchyard with a couple of stable hands from the hotel. They'd allowed they had the time, and he'd already noticed they had shovels.

Finding his way to the tombstone of the late Nathan Hemmings as they followed, Longarm pointed down and declared, "Like Brother Brigham said, this is the place. Like I told you, you'll find the 'dobe ain't been soaked and sun baked since they buried him."

One of the stable hands sank his shovel in the bare dirt mounded over the coffin far below and said, "You're right. It feels more like digging bird gravel. Almost as loose packed, least ways."

As the recruits began to get down to business they were naturally joined by others. It seemed you could hardly have a gunfight or dig up a grave in a small town without others coming over to ask what you thought you were doing.

Longarm saw Big Jim Tanner and young Pony Bodie, among others, as things got sort of crowded around the hog farmer's last resting place. So he said, "I wish you'd give us more room and be careful of them other graves, gents. How come so many of you are still packing guns?"

Pony Bodie replied, "I told you. We're on the prod for the persons unknown who cut up poor Preacher Shearer and his squaw."

Big Jim volunteered, "I keep telling the boys you shot the killer right next door. But who listens? Why are we exhuming poor old Nate, Deputy Long?"

Longarm said, "We ain't. I don't expect we'll have to dig down as far as the coffin lid. The killer wouldn't have had time to dig down more than a yard or so at the most."

The newspaperman demanded, "What killer? Gus Bergman? He wasn't in town when we buried the old timer in that grave."

Before Longarm had to answer one of his stable hands called out, "I've hit something soft and mushy here."

Longarm moved over to stare down at a scrap of flo-ral-print calico visible amid the dusty 'dobe clods and said, "Brush the dirt off her gentle, boys. She'd have wanted it that way."

So they did and soon had one arm, then a shoulder, then half the swollen face of the once-pretty Deputy Ida Weaver exposed to the cruel morning sun.

Somebody gasped. "Good Gawd! It's Ida Weaver!"

Somebody usually did.

Longarm said, "I wish folk didn't have to turn such funny colors after they were dead. It would be so much tidier if we could just dry up and blow away like faded flowers. But we don't. So pending an autopsy, I'd say they killed her as soon as she got home from Denver near to half a week ago."

"Do you have any idea who killed her?" asked Big Jim Tanner.

Longarm saw Rita Mae Reynolds coming over from her nearby house with her own gun strapped on, now, as he told the newspaperman it was too soon to say.

Rita rolled over the fence in her riding skirts and came over to take one look and gasp. "Oh, no! Not poor Ida! We were such good friends!"

Longarm said, "I'm sorry, ma'am. But that's what comes of sending inexperienced gals to carry out chores many a man would find too big a boo."

"But how could this have happened here in Keller's Crossing?" the auburn-haired bossy gal demanded, add-ing, "Ida *won* when she met up with that dangerous killer down in Denver, Custis!"

Longarm said, "Aw, he wasn't all that dangerous, next to some I've tangled with. Like Amarillo Cordwain, Texas Tom, and all them others, he was mostly too lazy to work and too dumb to cheat at cards. The one fairly experienced tinhorn they recruited lit out on them as soon as he saw how dumb they were acting."

Big Jim stared soberly down at the partly exposed cadaver of Ida Weaver to say, "Call them anything you like, as long as you bring them to justice! Why did you just say it was too soon to say? Do you have any idea at all who's behind all this?''

Longarm said, ''Sure. But you can't get milk out of a turtle just by trying to milk it, or a conviction out of a judge and jury just by pointing your finger with no proof.''

''What more proof do you need?'' asked Pony Bodie with a puzzled smile, pointing over at the nearby church as he said, ''That preacher played with fire until he got burnt. He was running some sort of home for wayward boys. But he felt he had to turn them in when they left home or robbed other folk or, shucks, he just got tired of them. He'd have been defrocked or worse had word gotten out that he went in for queer parties under his very own church. So, knowing Miss Rita, here, had a firmer way than most for dealing with outlaws, he saw she got tipped off they were outlaws, whether they were or not, and told her where they might be found, so's her deputy gals could finish them off for the old sneak!''

Longarm nodded thoughtfully as more than one in the crowd agreed that all made sense.

Longarm said, ''Well, like the old song says, farther along we'll know more about it. Your notion only adds up part way, Pony Bodie. I see how a dirty old man might use the law to aid and abet his fickle nature, or his worries about being blackmailed or exposed. But tell me how you think he got ten discarded lovers in a row to go where he wanted them to go and wait until he could sic the law on them.''

Pony Bodie looked confused.

Big Jim said, ''I might be able to answer that. You may have it backward. What if those double-gaited owl-hoot riders just left him, friendly or unfriendly. He told me he'd gotten wires from *others* he knew. Not as swishy lads of course. He told me he got to comfort and advise heaps of prairie drifters, good, bad, and indifferent. Couldn't he have simply put the word out on some former pal and waited until another wired him from wherever?''

Rita said, "That works for me. I'd heard Amarillo Cordwain had spent a lot of time in prison, getting known in the Biblical sense by a lot of other shady young men with no visible means of support."

Longarm said, "I've been thinking about that since first I found out about the preacher's other interests, Miss Rita. Not all the nine fugitives you and your wild deputies have accounted for had spent that much time in prison. Not all of them were thieves or robbers. So try her this way. What if somebody who knew about poor old Preacher Shearer and his rough-and-ready pansies was only using that angle to razzle-dazzle us with others?"

She said she didn't know what he was talking about.

He said, "It don't matter. I've been lying to you, too."

In the following silence he could have cut with a knife, Longarm explained, "I knew that once I got past Texas Tom and Ram Rogers, the survivors would be ordered to head somewhere else and await further instructions. I felt sure that once they arrived to be set up like clay pigeons, somebody was going to tell you where they were, so's you could send another wildwoman after them, no offense."

Rita gasped. "You did? Then why did you let me send that Covina Rivers from Cheyenne if you didn't want me to?"

Longarm said, "Oh, I wanted you to. That's how come I let you. Miss Covina was working with me. I asked her to. She lied to you herself. She never met Ram Rogers, and that shop gal she told you about was just a petty thief."

Rita looked hurt. "But why, Custis, why? I trusted you and I liked Covina! Why did you both lie to me?"

Longarm said, "I just told you she had orders to lie to you. I had to lie to everybody here, save for those pals from the hotel stable, least ways. I didn't know which one of you was behind all this dumb but deadly razzle-dazzle.''

"But you do now?" asked Big Jim warily.

Longarm hesitated, stepped back from the open grave a ways, and declared, "Not for certain, but likely by this afternoon. I'm waiting on a wire that ought to get here well before that last train out for the day. So the one I want ain't going nowheres before I'm ready to do some serious arresting around here!"

Rita asked, "Who's supposed to wire you about what? That Covina Rivers who ran off with one of our badges?"

Longarm smiled thinly and soothed, "I'll see you get your badge back, Miss Rita. I'll bet it's worth at least a dollar. I told Miss Covina just to go back to her notions store in Cheyenne and wait for her own compensations from my outfit. I know you told her to go down to Pueblo and flirt her way close enough to Ram Rogers to get the drop on him. I know you told her not to kill him if it could be avoided. So, to your credit, you and Judge Edith have commenced to behave more sensible."

He reached in his jacket for some matches and a cheroot as he continued, "Miss Covina wouldn't know Ram Rogers if she woke up in bed with him, and, after that, she's a lady who sells notions, not no manhunter. So I gave her a message to wire my own boss when she got to Cheyenne. It's been long sent by this time. My boss will be sending a team we call Smiley and Dutch down to Pueblo by now. Smiley and Dutch will take Ram Rogers alive if he knows what's good for him."

He lit a cheroot without offering in such a crowd and told them all, "Ram Rogers won't be sitting there waiting to be taken alive. The mastermind who's been advising him will have told him to go there and lay low pending further instructions. So he's going to be mighty chagrined when Smiley and Dutch tell him they were tipped off to his whereabouts by the one pal who'd be in any position to know."

Rita grinned like a kid who'd just spotted an unguarded apple tree and declared, "Then you've got him! He can't get away, and he's as good as in my jail the moment you hear from your friends in Pueblo!"

Longarm said, "That's about the size of it. Stay put, Miss Rita. I want to keep this private, and I see your words have inspired a certain nervousness over this way."

Then he snapped, "Don't do it, kid!" as Pony Bodie went for his Schofield .45, his weak-chinned face contorted with desperation!

The delivery boy was good, for a delivery boy or anybody else. Longarm would have been hard-pressed to beat the tensed-up killer to the draw if he hadn't been thinking ahead, himself.

But he had been. So he simply had to raise the right hand he'd been palming his derringer in and fire, point-blank, just as Pony Bodie's bigger gun was clearing leather.

The weak-chinned young terror staggered back against another tombstone, back-flipped over it, and landed facedown in the dust, sobbing as he struggled to rise with all that blood running out of his chest while Longarm held his double derringer's second round on him.

Then the treacherous young rascal collapsed limp as a bear rug left outside to air, and someone said, "I think you killed him."

Longarm said, "That was my intent. Like you all heard me tell him, getting a conviction can be a chore, and this way we won't have to air the dirty laundry of a lot of lesser sinners in these parts."

Rita marveled, "You mean you were lying to him, just to trick him?"

Longarm shrugged and answered truthfully, "I won't know until I hear from Smiley and Dutch. All I left out was that Smiley and Dutch can be wild as any Wyoming woman when you send 'em after a want. So I'll be pleasantly surprised if they take Ram Rogers alive. Not that it really matters, now."

Chapter 21

Longarm was more than pleasantly surprised by the long wire he got late that afternoon. For once the team of Smiley and Dutch had worked the way Billy Vail had planned when he put them to work together.

Deputy Smiley hardly ever smiled. Smiley was his last name and he was the smart but slower one. Nobody could pronounce the outlandish last name of the one they just called Dutch, but he was the fastest gun on the payroll, albeit about as levelheaded as a scorpion in one's empty boot of a morning. Billy's hope in teaming such an odd pair was that Dutch might keep Smiley alive while Smiley kept Dutch from being indicted for murder.

That hadn't always been easy for either of them. But the wire said they'd busted in on Ram Rogers and his ladylove at that Pueblo hotel to catch them in the act of posing for French postcards without any concealed weapons on them at all.

Smiley had thought to separate the two of them as soon as they were out of bed in their duds and handcuffs. They said Ram Rogers had been as chagrined as promised when they told him he'd been turned in by his Wyoming mastermind. The terrified gal, of course, had sung even louder when they got her to see she could tell all she knew or hope her true love would be waiting when she got out, old and gray.

The separately dictated statements of Ram Rogers and a gal called Rowdy Ruth agreed fairly well and cleared up loose ends Longarm hadn't managed to figure by himself. Billy Vail had ordered him to meet with county officials he hadn't gotten around to. But he didn't think his boss wanted him wasting the time, seeing there was nobody left to arrest and it was up to the voters, come November, whether they wanted the same bunch running things.

He could have caught the last night train out to save himself some time getting back to Cheyenne. But he reflected the railroading he'd want to detail in his officious report, and after that he owed Bronco Bob in Dwyer a borrowed mount and sadddle. He figured old Socks would be just as happy out on a moonlit prairie with him as moping in that livery across the street for days. So he left his room key on the bed upstairs and rode out of Keller's Crossing around suppertime, when he didn't have to bother about shaking hands with all creation.

Socks was happy to be loping into the sunset for home, and he let her have her head till they were past that drift fence and sailing over a rolling sea of tawny buffalo grass. But he didn't want to lather his mount with the literally cool shades of a Wyoming evening commencing to spread deep purple in the draws. So when they got to that cottonwood-lined creek, he reined her in and dismounted to water and rest her some, saying "We ain't in that big a hurry, Socks. You get me there by midnight, I'll still have to wait shivering on the platform for that night train to head back from Wendover, see?"

Socks just drank more creekwater. Longarm tethered her to a sapling, pissed on another one, and moved up the grassy slope away from any wood ticks to rest his ass by standing tall as he lit a cheroot.

Rita Mae Reynolds called out to ask if that was him when she spied his match flare from afar, aboard her own cordovan Morgan. Longarm had to identify himself to an undersheriff packing a pistol. So she loped on over, reined in, and slid gracefully from her sidesaddle to demand, "Why did you leave without saying goodbye? How could you leave me just hanging like that, you brute?"

Longarm said he hadn't known he was leaving her hanging. But when he took her in his arms to kiss her, she laughed wildly and gasped up at him, "I didn't mean you'd left me hanging *that* way! You were going to tell me all about poor Preacher Shearer and his outlaw gang and why he had Ida Weaver killed and—"

Longarm said, "You got that all wrong, Miss Rita. You were there when I had it out with the mastermind, one of them really dangerous crooks smart enough to let himself be taken for dumb and ornery enough to act harmless. I told you this morning that justice had been done and there was no call to hang a lot of dirty laundry out to dry over the graves of dead folk."

She kissed him, this time, and said, "Come and sit by my side in the grass and tell me all about it from the beginning."

So he did. As they reclined on the grassy slope in the gloaming he told her, "In the beginning God created man, then woman, then something more mixed up. Poor prim and scrawny Preacher Shearer was one of them mixed-up sorts. The army gives you a prison sentence and dishonorable discharge if they catch you behaving that way. The Indians allow some just can't help wanting to pretend they're gals, and so they let 'em. Indians almost never whip kids, neither. Sometime I get to wondering who's more Christian."

Rita said, "Big Jim told me all about the poor man being a queer. I can't for the life of me see what any man would get out of letting other men use him that way. Can you?''

Longarm said, ''I never spent that much time in jail. No man I've ever met has anything I'd be that interested in.''

She gasped. ''What do you think you're doing with that fresh hand? You told me you were going to tell me all about those queer outlaws!''

He lay her back in the grass and kissed her again but eased off when he felt her stiffen some. He said, ''I told you the villain was Pony Bodie. He assured me before I ever asked that he didn't go in for that sort of thing. That wasn't all he was fibbing about. He drifted into town a year or so back, as you may recall, fresh from an Alabama chain gang, which he forgot to tell any of you. He'd picked up bad habits in prison, and in no time at all he'd made friends with the only man in town who'd take the gal's part. He likely learned the preacher was prissy from some other saddle tramp. Poor old Shearer was too shy to ask gents such as Big Jim Tanner or the blacksmith.''

Rita giggled at that picture and didn't stiffen the next time he put a friendly hand on one firm breast, noticing she wore nothing at all under her whipcord riding habit. She asked him to go on. So he started to unbutton her bodice as he said, ''The preacher got his newfound secret lover a job delivering telegrams all over town for Western Union, with a chance to fiddle with the telegraph set late at night, acting the eager kid but having taken telegraph lessons in the reform school they'd tried on him first.''

He kissed her lightly as he ran his hand inside her bodice to find her nipples already turgid. He said, ''Remember Preacher Shearer didn't know this. He had no idea what Pony Bodie was up to behind his back, at first. His only crime was that he'd always wanted to be a pretty girl. Did anybody ever tell you how pretty your tits are in the soft light of gloaming, Miss Rita?''

She laughed and said, ''Many times. I was married to

a man who liked to sneak up on me, too. He had a drinking problem. Do I really need to say more?''

Longarm said, ''Nope. Once you say a man or woman has habits they can't control, you've about described them all, including the poor old preacher. That innocent beanpole with the goofy grin had the older man wrapped around his finger. Shearer got him a job, gave him money from the poor box, and begged for more abuse from Pony Bodie and his pals.''

She said, ''Down, boy, you're moving in on me too fast, and I thought you said there was no gang.''

Longarm left his free hand on her inner thigh, having established she wasn't wearing one of those infernal split skirts that could make it awkward as hell as you worked up a gal's inner thigh, and repeated, ''Preacher Shearer was never in charge. He didn't know what Pony Bodie was getting him into until a whole mess of disgusting young owlhoot riders had taken to getting into him and hiding out under his church lest you or one of your kid deputies ask them what they were doing in your township.''

She asked, ''What were they doing? Oh, Custis, what's that *you're* doing, you naughty thing?''

''Just trying to have a friendly conversation,'' he replied as he parted her pubic hair wider to cradle her moist clit between the tips of two fingers, adding, ''What *they* were doing was as much petty crime as they could get away with with Pony Bodie scouting for them as a delivery boy who traipsed all over, delivering money orders, overhearing gossip, and so on. As he started to get bolder he was still stuck with splitting the spoils or double-crossing pals close to his home base and having real messes to clean up, even if he won.''

''Could you tell me the rest after you make me come, dear?'' she cut in, coyly admitting, ''I guess you know I've been hearing things about you and other lonely widows, grass or veiled.''

So he shoved her skirts up out of the way and rolled into the wide welcome of her athletic bare thighs while she unbuckled his gun belt and helped him get his jeans down a piece after he'd entered her. Then she was begging him to take it out while she wrapped her long legs around him, thrusting her pelvis higher. Longarm was too delicate to observe that any poor simp who'd gotten drunk when he had something like this to enjoy had his total sympathy. He just acceded to her request as graciously as he knew how when she got to yelling, "Oh, yesss! Deeper! Harder! I've had to watch out for my reputation, and it's been so long and you're so long and, my God, I've never come this sooooon!"

Longarm had been in bed with sweet little Inky more recently than Rita had been with anybody, judging by the way she was chewing on him with her soft wet innards. So he got her to come thrice in the time it took him to feel the need for a smoke while he caught his second wind.

He'd lost track of that first cheroot he'd lit. It hadn't started a prairie fire under them. So he figured it was safe to light up one more and, while they had the time, strip down to the buff and sprawl friendly atop their duds in the springy but pricklesome dry grass.

As they did so, Longarm remembered his manners and said, "You and your girlish deputies gave Pony Bodie the grand notion how he could get rich. Neither he nor his transient trash had anything to do with them first three wants you had your gals bring back dead instead of alive. They read about it in the *Riverside News*. Big Jim's only crime was a tendency to make mountains out of molehills. The way more modest Pony Bodie talked, an old boy laying over with Preacher Shearer, while laying him, to hold up that cattle buyer staying at the Pronghorn across the street from the Western Union. After pointing the victim out, Pony Bodie sat there spitting and whittling in front of everybody while the deed was done, gave you all a false description of the masked man fleeing the scene, and met him later under the church."

She said, "That would have been the late Trigger

Woods we caught up with in Missouri, right?''

He said, ''You *thought* you caught up with him. Pony Bodie talked his old reform-school pal into leaving the loot with him for safekeeping and wiring for it once he got to a safe hideout.''

Rita said, ''Good Lord! Were all of them that dumb! Why didn't any of the others tumble to his simple duplicity as soon as we began to get those tips from the rascal they'd wired for their money?''

Longarm passed her the cheroot as he told her, ''You never got one tip from Pony Bodie. I don't know what he told Preacher Shearer, but Preacher Shearer would tell Big Jim, and Big Jim would puff out his chest and tell you. I still don't like him. But I don't have any more hard feeling for the *Riverside News* right now. Counting that serious stage holdup, when Rusty Mansfield scared the whole bunch by gunning Miss Ida Weaver's uncle, they pulled off a half dozen serious crimes and would have been caught sooner if other pests hadn't convinced my boss and me we were up against a bigger mystery than there really was.''

As she moved his hand back where she liked it, Longarm told her, ''Everything went according to plan up to where Ida Weaver gunned Rusty Mansfield and the Denver papers reported I was mixed up in it. Bodie wired Rowdy Ruth, a Denver harlot he'd spent some time with for the novelty, and asked her to watch me. When she reported Ida and me had been to the federal building, Bodie put two and two together and came up with three. He hadn't used Ram Rogers up yet. So he ordered Ram to see if he could stop me from getting warm, and Ram recruited the older Texas Tom and Deacon Knox to blur the pattern for me some.''

Rita sighed and said, ''I feel so bad about poor Ida. You think they killed her because they feared Rusty Mansfield had told her something as he lay dying?''

Longarm nodded and said, ''It would have been easy. Bodie could have met her train and offered to walk her up to your place in the dark. He stabbed her and buried

179

her in fresh-dug 'dobe when he had her alone up by the churchyard.''

He took the cheroot back for a drag and went on, ''Nobody did anything all that clever. They had me thinking I was playing a smarter game because rascals too dumb to beat me at checkers kept showing me independent dumb moves that I kept trying to string together. Making a personal enemy along the way didn't help. That poor crazy Swede was after me and me alone. But after I'd made it past Rogers and company in Cheyenne, Gus Bergman did me an unintended favor when he drew my attention to that church and churchyard by sniping at us from the best really high point handy. Bodie thought I was getting warm on purpose. So he figured it was time to close shop and hide his own tracks. He sent Rogers and Rowdy Ruth to a swell hideout. So he'd know where they were when he had Shearer tell Tanner who'd surely tell you where they were. He hoped you'd send somebody wilder than Smiley and Dutch.''

They'd gotten to where they could read each other's body movements without having to jaw about it. So Longarm took her up on her unspoken invite and rolled back in her love saddle as he added, ''After that he figured he only had to murder Shearer, who had to have known too much, and that old Indian gal, who might have known all or nothing at all. I see no point in speaking ill of the dead.''

Rita wrapped her thighs around him to croon, ''I've nothing ill to say about that poor crazy Swede bringing things to a head so soon. I don't see how we'd have ever gotten up the nerve to behave this wild back in town, darling.''

To which Longarm replied, moving his rump faster as the stars came out to admire it, ''Aw, we'd have thought of something.''

Watch for

**LONGARM AND THE
DURANGO DOUBLE-CROSS**

231st novel in the exciting LONGARM series
from Jove

Coming in March!

BUSHWHACKERS

First in an all-new series from the creators of Longarm!

They were the most brutal gang of cutthroats ever assembled. And during the Civil War, they sought justice outside of the law—paying back every Yankee raid with one of their own. They rode hard, shot straight, and had their way with every willin' woman west of the Mississippi. No man could stop them. No woman could resist them. And no Yankee stood a chance of living when Quantrill's Raiders rode into town...

Win and Joe Coulter become the two most wanted men in the West. And they learn just how sweet—and deadly— revenge could be...